MISTS OF DARKNESS

Who tried to kill TV producer Zannah Edgecumbe by pushing her over a cliff? The answer is hidden somewhere in her slowly returning memory. Is it cameraman Jonathan Tyler, her aggressive and passionate fiancé, or is it Matthew Tregenna, the handsome but remote doctor treating her — the man with whom she is falling in love? She remembers Hugh, the boy she adored as a child — but where is he now? Lost in an abyss of blurred and broken memories, Zannah must return to the cliff-top to discover the horrifying truth.

REBECCA BENNETT

◆

MISTS OF DARKNESS

Complete and Unabridged

LINFORD
Leicester

First published in Great Britain in 1989

First Linford Edition
published 2016

Copyright © 1989 by Rebecca Bennett
All rights reserved

A catalogue record for this book is available
from the British Library.

ISBN 978–1–4448–2764–4

T. J. International Ltd., Padstow, Cornwall

This book is printed on acid-free paper

1

'Hello there. So you've decided to come back to us at last.'

A man stood, almost filling the doorway with his height. Intense blue eyes gazed down at me from a square-chinned, suntanned face. Thick black hair hung over his broad forehead in an untidy sweep. His smiling mouth was wide and generous.

With long, easy strides he moved towards the bed, hands tucked into the pockets of his unbuttoned white coat, a worried look on his face as he bent over me, taking my wrist in gentle fingers.

'This is Doctor Tregenna,' explained the nurse, her face, dark against the starched whiteness of her cap, smiling down at me.

'Matthew Tregenna.' His voice was deep and resonant with a warm Cornish note.

But how did I know it was Cornish, when everything else was a blank?

'Please call me Matthew,' he said. 'We don't stand on ceremony here. Now, tell me your name.'

I tried to answer, but my voice was dry and hoarse, every word hurting my throat.

'I . . . don't . . . know.'

'You don't know?' Surprise filled his eyes.

'A fall like that could make her lose her memory, Doctor,' reasoned the nurse.

'It's not unusual, I suppose. She is badly concussed. And in shock as well,' he agreed, directing his conversation to the nurse as if I wasn't there at all.

Then, with a slight apologetic smile, he turned to me. 'Never mind. Everything will come back to you in a couple of days, I feel sure. Now, the first thing to do is get you better — and that means complete rest. No visitors, Nurse. She's under your care.'

2

No visitors, I thought. How could there be? Without a name, who could one tell? Who would even know I was here?

Just the effort of those few minutes talking with Doctor Tregenna had left me exhausted and I slept again.

★　★　★

It was dark when I woke, a small shaded lamp glowing on the table beside my bed. Someone was leaning over me, shadowy in the dim light, gazing intently down at me. For a second pulsing terror surged through me, stiffening my body into a rigid board of fear, then as Matthew Tregenna spoke, I relaxed.

'Hello,' he whispered gently, his eyes full of kindness.

I smiled, feeling the drag of the bandages as I did so.

'How's that memory?'

I shook my head ruefully.

He pulled up a chair and sat down,

his thick dark hair flopping over his eyes as he leaned forward to talk to me.

'Tell me everything you can remember. Would you like some water first?'

'Please,' I said gratefully.

He held a spouted cup to my lips and I sipped it, feeling the dryness of my throat ease a little.

'Better? Now let's try and remember.'

★　★　★

. . . A harebell quivered, fragile and blue. Above, the sky was hazy. Seagulls hovered there on silent wings. I could hear the sound of waves pounding. Drifts of spray misted my cheeks.

Cautiously I moved my hand over tussocks of stiff dry grass — then touched nothing.

I was on a ledge, just wide enough to hold me, the grass cushioning my body. Far below, the sea crashed over jagged rocks, while above, far above, I could see clouds drifting, white and nebulous.

A tiny ledge, holding and supporting

me, far above the sea. *But how did I get there?*

My brain was hazy, like the sky. Confused. Bewildered. Thoughts struggled through slowly, but I didn't know the answers.

Where was I?

Who was I?

The sun grew hotter, burning down on my face and bare arms. I tried to cover my eyes from its glare. Ragged pain tore into me and a rush of darkness closed round me like a cloak.

★   ★   ★

When I opened my eyes again the sun was high, a dazzle of brightness blazing onto me. A trickle of sweat ran down my body, weaving its way slowly between my breasts and creeping round to my back. But when I raised my head, the pain was so intense I slid back into oblivion.

★   ★   ★

The sun had moved now, hanging low in the sky, reaching out long fingers of scarlet across the azure surface of the sea. Soon it would disappear, slipping down beneath the edge of the horizon, bringing the cold harsh darkness of night. Already I could feel its chill.

Desperation flooded over me as I cried out, but only the echo of my voice came back, thin and weak. No one could hear me.

No one was there.

★　★　★

There was a flapping sound. Something brushed my arm. I opened weary eyes.

Resting on my chest was a tangle of scarlet and bits of thin, shattered wood. For a second I was puzzled, until I realised what it was.

A kite. A child's kite, its fine string broken and dangling. That must mean . . .

I looked up, my eyes desperately searching the darkening skyline at the

6

top of the cliff. Could I hear voices; or was it only the cry of the gulls, wheeling and dipping, as they returned to the cliffs to roost?

'Help me,' I croaked, through dry lips. 'Please, please help me.'

★   ★   ★

The sun was a rosy glow now, illuminating the grey of the sea, when a whisper of sound filled the air, growing like the murmur of bees.

Nearer and nearer, louder and louder until the cliffs echoed with the noise, deafening me. With a roar it rose to a crescendo of resonance, surrounding me with its intensity, vibrating the tiny ledge on which I lay.

A helicopter. Black and sonorous.

Wind whirled round me, seizing the kite and tossing it high into the sky. I watched it tremble for a second, then drop, imagining its downward spiralling flight, to be seized by the waves and snatched away.

Something snaked downwards towards me, followed by the dark figure of a man, hanging like a spider on its thread, twisting and turning.

A face appeared close to mine. A voice, deep yet soothing.

'You're safe now, love.'

Strong hands gripped me. Pain radiated through me, engulfing me. For a brief second I felt myself swung into a void, the calm voice still echoing in my ears.

The sun had vanished now and the sky was bathed in a fiery glow as I hung there, suspended in endless time, then velvety darkness surrounded me . . .

★   ★   ★

'There was a ledge,' I said. 'On the cliff.'

'Can you remember anything before that?' Doctor Tregenna prompted gently.

I thought carefully, trying to penetrate that dense barrier obscuring my reluctant mind.

8

'Nothing,' I replied at last.

'But how did you get on the ledge? Surely you must know that? Did you fall? Slip? The cliff path is very treacherous up there.'

I could only remember the brightness of the sun and the softness of the grass beneath my body as I lay there. Beyond that, nothing at all.

'What about your name?'

I must have a name, but what?

'Let's try a few and see if any one triggers off a reaction,' he said, reaching out to take my hand, his fingers curling round it, strong and firm, and gentle.

My eyes were heavy with sleep and his voice drifted hazily around me, but none of the names he spoke meant anything at all.

'Let's try some more . . . '

I closed my eyes and slept.

★   ★   ★

The sun shone bright, emphasising the plain whiteness of the room. Kati, my nurse, was putting a breakfast tray on the table at the side of my bed.

'You look a better colour this morning — from the little I can see of your face,' she said, her strong white teeth gleaming against the darkness of her skin as she smiled.

Despite the dull ache in my limbs and body, I did feel a lot better, all the numbing exhaustion gone. Suddenly I felt hungry and began to tuck into the scrambled eggs Kati had brought for me, chewing with tiny cautious bites. My jaw was still tender.

'Can I have a mirror?' I asked, when I'd finished.

'Aha! You are feeling better,' grinned Kati, 'but you might not like what you see,' she warned, holding a hand mirror in front of me.

I stared back at my reflection in horror. Black thread stood out starkly against the smooth tanned skin of my forehead and dark bruises shadowed my cheeks. My hair was drawn severely away from my face, leaving it gaunt and ugly. Had I ever been pretty? I wondered.

'You've suffered some concussion and fractured your right arm, but really you're very lucky. Falling down a cliff like that should have spelt death. The rocks at the bottom are lethal, apart from the treacherous currents round there. If it hadn't been for that ledge, you definitely would have been killed.'

The meaning of Kati's words swept over me, her wide brown eyes staring into mine, full of curiosity.

'I wonder how on earth I fell,' I mused thoughtfully.

'Fell?' cried Kati. 'You didn't fall. From the bruises on your arms, someone gripped you very tightly and pushed you over that cliff. Someone was trying to kill you.'

'Get out of this room!'

Matthew Tregenna stood by the door, his face sharp with anger. 'How dare you talk to a patient like that, Nurse. I told you she is to have rest and quiet. What do you mean by upsetting her with your stupid remarks?'

Kati's dark eyes flooded with tears at the raw fury in his voice.

'I'm sorry, Doctor Tregenna, I didn't think . . . '

'Didn't think? How long have you worked here? Surely you must know by now that the patient's welfare comes first. In future keep any foolish and ridiculous ideas you may have to yourself, Nurse. Do you understand that?'

Kati nodded her head and turned quickly to leave the room.

'I apologise for that outburst,' Matthew said, taking my hand in his and letting his fingers move, backwards and forwards, with a pleasing, soothing action.

'Is Kati right? Was I thrown over the cliff?' I demanded, clutching anxiously at his sleeve.

His lips tightened and an angry pulse beat in his cheek. 'You could have been,' he replied cautiously.

'My arms are bruised like she said?' I questioned.

'There are bruises,' he agreed.

'And my other injuries?'

'You fell a considerable distance. Even landing on soft grass would produce some damage.'

'Do you believe someone threw me over the cliff?' I persisted.

'As I said before, it's possible, but I doubt it,' he answered brusquely. 'Now, let's have a look at you this morning. You definitely seem a lot brighter. You're talking more easily too. What about the memory?'

I shook my head slightly, wincing at the movement.

'Nothing?' he asked.

'Nothing.'

'Well, someone must be missing you,' he said, raising the third finger of my left hand.

I glanced down, noticing for the first time the clear white mark in my suntan. Matthew Tregenna produced a ring from his pocket and slipped it back on

13

my finger, staring down at it with an unfathomable look in his blue eyes.

'Sapphires and diamonds. Very expensive too, I should imagine. It looks as though you're engaged to quite a wealthy man. Now, does that bring back any memories?'

I gazed down at the ring sparkling in the bright sunshine that filled the room, desperately searching my brain, but it was as if a dense curtain hung there, shrouding everything I'd ever known.

'Never mind,' comforted Doctor Tregenna. 'Something will trigger off that elusive past of yours eventually. It could take hours, or even days — but I want to make quite sure I'm around when it does return. It's not every day I have such a beautiful and mysterious patient. You intrigue me.'

His fascinating eyes smiled down at me as he spoke. Reluctantly I let my hand slip from his grasp and watched his tall figure stride purposefully towards the door.

2

The ring was a dazzle of brilliance as I lay there, twisting it this way and that on my finger, hoping just looking at it would bring back some recollection of the man who had given it to me.

Rainbows of colour shimmered out from the four diamonds surrounding the inky-blue depths of an enormous square-cut sapphire in their midst. An expensive ring, Matthew Tregenna had said, to show the love someone held for me.

But who? If someone loved me so much, why couldn't I remember?

Kati's worried dark face peeped cautiously round the door.

'Has he gone?' she whispered, her huge round eyes still wet with tears. 'I'm sorry — I really didn't mean to upset you. It's just that . . . it's all a bit strange. You were thrown or pushed,

I'm quite sure about that. I've seen finger-mark bruises like those before — on some of the battered wives I nursed during my training. They're unmistakable. Someone gripped your arms. And very violently too.'

'What is this place?' I questioned, wanting to change the subject. Kati's words were beginning to frighten me.

'Tolruan? It's a private nursing-home, very close to where you were found. The nearest hospital is several miles away and very short-staffed with all the strikes. The rescue crew couldn't be sure just how bad your injuries were. They thought you'd fractured your spine, so it was vital to get attention quickly for you. And Doctor Tregenna has the best and most up-to-date equipment in this part of Cornwall, which is why they brought you here,' she said proudly.

'Does he own Tolruan?' I asked in surprise.

'For the time being,' answered Kati ruefully. 'But for how much longer, we don't know. It's an expensive place to run and we don't seem to have many wealthy patients. Doctor Tregenna will insist on taking in people who are desperate for treatment — regardless of whether they can actually pay for it. He's a fantastic doctor and devoted to his work, but that doesn't cope with the bills, I'm afraid. Things are looking pretty black at the moment and he's desperate not to lose the place.'

She smoothed the covers tidily over my bed and moved the pillows to a more comfortable position.

'Now you should be resting, not talking. I'll be in more trouble with Doctor Tregenna if you don't get some sleep.'

I gazed down at the ring again, searching deep into my mind, a myriad of iridescent colour dazzling my eyes until they grew heavy — and closed.

* * *

. . . The fringed edge of the brightly coloured red and green tartan blanket

troubled me and I straightened each fat strand, laying it carefully smooth against the sand. Beside me I could see the skirt of her cotton dress, brilliant with scattered scarlet poppies on a white background. One suntanned foot was curled under her. The other stretched onto the softness of the sand, her toes bare like my own. I felt the warmth of her love surrounding me like the blanket, safe and comforting.

Across the wide expanse of beach I could see the boy, leaning over some rocks, peering deep into a pool. His long thin legs were patterned with damp sand, clinging; the hem of his fawn shorts wet from the sea. Above them the knobs of his spine stood out like a row of shiny pebbles. Thick dark tousled hair hung round his face, hiding it from me.

I wanted to be there, next to him, my arm touching his, looking into the rock pool, seeing what he saw.

'No,' came her warning voice and her restraining hand caught the straps of *my pink candy-striped sundress, pulling me back onto the rug. 'Let him be, child. He's lost in a world of his own. Poor little scrap's tormented enough, without having a little girl like you bothering him as well.'*

There was no unkindness in her voice as she gently stroked my long hair, only a tinge of sadness.

'Please,' I begged, seeing the boy's head turn towards me . . .

★   ★   ★

Matthew Tregenna sat by the side of my bed, his eyes distant and far away.

'Awake?'

I smiled up at him, glad he was there. It was a day or so later and, apart from the devastating blankness of my mind, I felt quite fit and well again.

'Today, I think a little fresh air is called for. You've been cooped up here for far too long. Sitting out there on the balcony isn't enough.'

He smiled, his face becoming almost

boyish as it changed from formality. 'Occasionally I allow myself an afternoon off and as the sun is shining, how about coming down to the sea with me for a while?'

'I'd love that,' I cried eagerly.

The lines of tiredness round his eyes eased as he laughed.

'Don't get too enthusiastic. You might find yourself a bit wobbly when you try. See you in ten minutes then.'

I looked round for my clothes and found them placed neatly on a chair, noticing that they'd been newly washed. The faded lavender blue tee-shirt was smooth and soft, my jeans freshly ironed. As quickly as I could I slipped into them, the plaster cast on my arm making my movements awkward.

Doctor Tregenna was waiting in the corridor when I looked out, no longer wearing his formal crisp white coat. Casual fawn linen trousers covered his long legs and a blue check shirt, open at the neck, emphasised the breadth of his shoulders. He took my arm and led me down a wide curving wooden staircase into the hallway.

'It's just like a stately home,' I gasped, gazing round in wonder.

'Tolruan is a fourteenth-century manor house,' he said, his face lighting up with obvious enthusiasm. 'It's a beautiful place, don't you think?'

I nodded in agreement.

Outside I climbed into his car and we drove down a long avenue of beech trees, past open green fields. I looked back at the lovely grey-stone house, half-hidden amongst bright flowering shrubs and smooth green lawns. No wonder Matthew wanted to keep it so much. It was ideal for a nursing-home; remote, peaceful and beautiful.

Matthew slowed the car to go past the tall wrought-iron scrollwork of the gates, then we moved out into the road, following it over downland thick with yellow gorse, winding down narrow lanes until in the distance I could see the sea glinting in the sunshine.

Carefully Matthew guided the car

through a gap in the hedge into a field scattered with parked cars. A thin brown-skinned boy in faded denim shorts stood by the entrance, collecting the money and handing over a small scrap of paper as a ticket.

'No multi-storeys here I'm afraid,' Matthew smiled, stopping the car and switching off the engine.

He led the way along a well-trodden path beside the hedge, to the other side of the field and helped me over a wooden stile, then on down a twisting narrow lane to a cluster of tiny shops.

'I think all the local inhabitants spend their winter months making these strange novelties,' he said, pointing to lamps and bowls made of an unusual stone.

'It's serpentine,' he explained, noticing my puzzled stare. 'The local rock round this part of the coast. You can just see the difference in colour — a sort of greenish shade — from the grey-brown granite in most parts of Cornwall.'

We clambered over the rocks to the edge of the sea, and I stopped for a second, beginning to feel rather breathless. Matthew gave me an anxious glance.

'Let's sit down. I was worried you might find all this a bit tiring. Would you rather go back to the car?'

'Oh no,' I cried hastily. 'I'm fine.' But I sank gratefully onto a smooth rock all the same.

'Do you mind if I swim? It's about the only chance for exercise I have, so I like to make the most of it whenever I get the opportunity.'

Matthew was unbuttoning his shirt as he spoke, to show a lean deeply tanned body, matted with dark hair. I watched him with undisguised admiration as he slipped out of his pale linen trousers, revealing a pair of dark blue bathing trunks. On strong muscular legs, he splashed into the water and began to swim with firm steady strokes.

I rested my back against the rock, feeling the sun burn into my skin, suddenly content. Who I was, where I was didn't seem to matter any more. Only that I was here with Matthew.

A spatter of water startled me and he was standing above me, rubbing his lithe body with a thick striped towel, his teeth chattering slightly.

'It's absolutely freezing!' he shivered, standing on one leg to dry his toes.

'You'll soon warm up. The sun's baking.'

I felt the chill of his arm brush mine as he sank onto the rocks beside me. Through half-closed eyes I watched him, seeing a tiny drop of water meander slowly through the tangle of darkness matting his chest and disappear into the deep hollow of his navel. His hair clung to his head, sleek like a seal, outlining the shape of his face. He wasn't good-looking in the traditional sort of way. His eyes were too large; his nose craggy; his mouth wide. And yet, looking at him filled me with an acute sense of longing.

As if aware, he opened one clear blue

eye and met my stare with a hint of challenge. I felt my cheeks burn — but it wasn't from the sun.

'Relax. Make the most of today. They aren't all like this, you know. It can be a bleak place at times,' he smiled.

I settled myself contentedly beside him and let my eyes close.

★ ★ ★

. . . I was splashing through the shallow water, bending, searching, my heavy plait of hair falling over one shoulder. Then I saw it. A bright yellow shell. Seizing it in my hand, I ran quickly up the beach to where they sat talking, heads close, one dark, one grey; hers bent low over his.

'Here she comes, the little love,' came her rich warm voice as she stood up to wrap me in a soft towel and hug me.

I struggled from its encircling folds to peep over her shoulder at the boy sitting hunched beside her, his knees pulled up to his chin, eyes glowering back at me from under that thick fringe of hair.

'Look what I found for you, Hugh,' I cried triumphantly, holding out the shell . . .

3

'Hugh!'

Matthew's head jerked towards me, his dark eyes wide and startled.

'The boy,' I said. 'The boy on the beach.'

He looked around him, puzzled. 'What boy?'

'I don't know, but I remember him, there on the beach, with her.'

'Who?'

'I never see her face. I just know she's there, radiating warmth and love . . . I can't explain.'

Tears were beginning to brim in my eyes and slide down my cheeks. A terrible feeling of desolation flooded over me.

'Everything was safe then. That's all I know.'

Matthew's hand reached out and took mine, his fingers lightly stroking it with a soothing movement.

'This boy,' he said. 'Tell me about him.'

'All I know is that he's so lonely,' I replied, frowning as I tried to remember. 'Withdrawn, shut off from everyone — and yet I love him so much and want to comfort him. Oh, I can't explain, Matthew, but it's as if he desperately needs people, but won't let anyone get close to him.'

Matthew's expression was very serious as he gazed back at me, searching and delving into my mind, trying to plumb its depths.

'And his name is Hugh?'

I nodded bleakly. 'I think so.'

'Think so? Aren't you sure?'

'That's the name that comes into my mind, whenever I remember him. It must be his. Perhaps he's my brother. He's someone very close to me, I'm quite certain of that.'

I leaned back against the rock and closed my eyes, letting the sun's comforting warmth seep into me, hearing the splash of waves as they foamed over the beach; feeling the peace.

A vision of the boy floated back into my head, seeing him once more, sitting there, tight and angry beside her, refusing to take the shell I offered him.

★ ★ ★

. . . 'Take no notice, my lovely,' her warm voice whispered in my ear as I stared in miserable bewilderment at Hugh. 'He doesn't really mean to hurt you, but he's so tangled up inside, so confused, poor mite.'

I watched him leap to his feet and run down to the edge of the sea, to stand there, angrily throwing pebbles into the waves, his thin brown back stiff and straight.

Her hands were drying my arms with the towel as she spoke, sand prickling into them.

'Now that his mother has married again, he just can't accept the new man in her life. We must try and be kind to *him, lovey, whatever he does. He's so sad and lonely.'*

'Like the stone frog?' I asked her.

Her face creased into deep lines of laughter and she gave me a hug, kissing the dampness of my hair.

'Just like the stone frog, my darling.' . . .

★ ★ ★

'The stone frog.'

I sat up suddenly, gripping Matthew's arm.

'Stone frog? What do you mean?'

'Oh, Matthew. I don't know, I really don't know anything any more,' I wailed in despair. 'Everything's churning and twisting in my brain like a whirlpool. Every so often something rises to the surface like a bubble. Little bursts of memory — but none of them mean anything to me at all.'

'They will, they will,' Matthew soothed, bending his dark head towards mine.

His nearness surrounded me, drawing me to him. A strand of his hair brushed my brow. I could smell the salt of the sea on his skin. Feel the warmth of his breath. See the haunting depths of his blue eyes as he leaned towards me, his mouth almost touching mine. Then, with a swift movement, he jerked away, his eyes remote once more.

'Let's go and see the lighthouse,' he said abruptly, rising to his feet, scattering dry sand from his long tanned legs.

He bent to pull me to my feet, his face close to mine once more, but the magic was gone. A tenseness drew his mouth into a thin line and the muscles of his cheeks were taut.

We clambered over the rocks and climbed to the top of the cliffs, where the runway of the old lifeboat-station stretched down to the beach.

People sat in the sunshine outside a café drinking cups of tea and eating cream-covered scones, heaped with jam. Wasps darted round them, brushed away by frantic hands.

A small queue waited outside the souvenir shop, faces pressed close to the windows, fingers pointing, eagerly choosing, changing mind, and choosing again.

We followed a narrow track round the side of the cliff, seeing the sea lap gently far down at its base, tiny pale-blue butterflies hovering over the brilliance of multicoloured flowers clinging to the steep slopes.

A soft breeze ruffled the stiff tussocks of grass when we reached the gate of the lighthouse, and I stopped breath-lessly to gaze up at the dazzling white tower high above us.

'Can you manage the steps?' asked Matthew. 'Or shall we not go up? I'm getting worried about you overdoing things, you know.'

'I'm fine,' I insisted. 'And I certainly don't want to miss anything. The view from the top must be fantastic.'

We waited with half a dozen people — an elderly couple from the north of

England; a lively little boy of about three or four years old, his parents trying unsuccessfully to keep him still, and a tall bronzed Australian curious to discover the Cornish way of life.

When the first tour ended, the lighthouse-keeper came to collect us. He looked doubtfully at my plastered arm with a twinkle of humour in his deep-set eyes.

'Have you been here before?' he joked. 'The other keeper's a very ferocious man, always throwing people off the top.'

The others laughed, eyeing my arm with amusement, but my legs trembled at his ill-chosen words.

Matthew was close behind me, his arm holding the rail, supporting my back, while we climbed the steep stone steps that changed to narrow metal ones, clanging loudly with our hollow footsteps as we went higher.

Slowly we all inched into the tower, and stood crowded closely together round the massive light, a faint throat-catching smell of polish hanging in the air from the gleaming brasswork. The small boy struggled to see and his father lifted him high onto his shoulders, where he perched, warily clinging with tight hands to the man's perspiring forehead.

I could feel the sun burn onto the nape of my neck through the curved windows surrounding us and turned to look out into the hazy distance as the keeper's deep tones droned on.

' . . . thirty miles on a clear day. That's as far as you can see to the horizon.'

A sea-going yacht bobbed its way, snowy sails billowing. Beyond that a tanker, rust showing orange against the whiteness of its bow.

' . . . floating on a bed of mercury. See how easily it turns . . . '

The light revolved slightly and I followed the movement, with my eyes travelling to the edge of the cliff where it jutted out over the clear blue of the sea.

' . . . and that is the famous Lizard

Rock from which the point gets its name . . . '

I looked in the direction the keeper was indicating — and my heart began to pound, sunshine searing and blazing round me from the dazzle of brasswork. A swirling quiver of mist began to distort my vision.

Perched on an outcrop of flat dark rock was the stone frog.

'Are you all right?' Matthew's voice echoed hollowly near my ear as I clutched desperately at his sleeve.

'The heat's got at her,' came a woman's voice.

'Shouldn't have come up here with her arm like that,' muttered another. 'Asking for trouble on a hot day like this.'

My vision cleared slightly and I began to breathe deeply, my eyes fixed on the rock shape.

I'd always called it the stone frog. It still didn't look like a lizard to me.

4

We were the last to descend the narrow staircase from the top of the lighthouse. Matthew placed a steadying hand on either side of my waist guiding me, as he led the way down, facing inwards to the steep steps. My fingers slid clammily over the cold metal of the handrail.

'I shouldn't have taken you up there. It was a stupid thing to do,' he apologised. 'I'm sorry.'

'There's nothing to apologise for, Matthew. I wanted to go. It was my choice. And, anyway, I'm fine now,' I assured him, only too thankful to be breathing sharp salt air once more as the warm breeze rippled round us.

'We'll go and have a cup of tea. It'll make you feel better. Then it's straight back to Tolruan,' Matthew said, taking my hand in his and I felt my own quiver in his strong clasp.

Returning to the café on the cliffs, we sat at a round white-painted metal table, with a large striped umbrella fluttering over our heads.

'Cream tea, m'dears?' enquired the plump little waitress, wiping the table clean of crumbs in one swift movement.

Matthew looked at me and raised one eyebrow in question.

'Why not?' he said. 'Two cream teas please.'

The woman smiled happily and bustled away, easing her ample body deftly between the tables.

I gazed out over the low wall. Seaweed hung in black trails from the rocks, appearing like shadows under the deep blue of the sea. A row of shags perched, dark and sinister, on a tiny islet; one suddenly rising to fly low over the surface of the water, then dive, its thin neck jerking convulsively as it swallowed a fish.

Matthew cut my scones for me and piled on jam and cream, then poured the strong tea into our cups, his face intent as he concentrated on preventing a dribble of liquid running back from the spout.

'Was it the heat up there in the lighthouse or is your arm troubling you?' he asked, regarding me with anxious eyes.

I hesitated, biting deep into the thick cream and savouring the tangy sharpness of the strawberry jam.

'No . . . ' I replied slowly.

'Then what?'

'The Lizard Rock,' I said, still feeling an uneasy sense of strangeness.

'You remembered seeing it before?'

I nodded. 'Yes, but I didn't call it that. I always thought it was a frog. It must have been a long, long time ago, when I was a child. I suppose I'd never seen a lizard — didn't know what one looked like — but there were frogs in the pond.'

I stopped, aware of a sudden alertness in his gaze.

'Go on,' he prompted, stirring sugar

into his tea. 'The pond . . . '

'There was a pond — with lilies. Pink lilies, looking like wax. And a yellowy-brown frog used to sit there sometimes . . . all alone. Just like the Lizard Rock out there on the point.' I reached out to clasp his hand and felt his fingers tighten round mine. 'I know it so well, Matthew. I must have been here many times before.'

'We must go back to Tolruan now. It is only your first time out.' Matthew smiled down into my eyes. 'You're making good progress but I don't want you to overdo things by trying too hard.'

'Oh please let's stay a little while longer. I'm fine now. Really I am,' I begged. 'It was rather a shock though — seeing it again like that.'

I turned to Matthew eagerly. 'It's the first time something tangible has actually triggered off my memory, isn't it? Surely that must be a good sign?'

Matthew didn't answer but sat,

drinking his tea and staring thought-fully out to sea, watching the shags sit motionless on their rocky island.

'Can we walk on a bit? It's so beautiful here. Please say yes, Matthew.'

'Not far then. Just to that seat up there on the cliffs. No further. I really should be taking you home.'

I brushed crumbs from my jeans and stood up, quite recovered now and ready to walk over the springy turf.

We made our way along the narrow well-trodden cliff path, seeing the depths of the sea glint and sparkle like a night sky filled with stars, stepping sideways when we met other people coming towards us, to let them pass.

I leaned against the wooden gate of a cottage while a stream of chattering small girls in Brownie uniform skipped by, the two plump perspiring ladies in charge, calling out words of warning — 'Not too near the edge' — as the adventurous ones roved on ahead.

A 'For Sale' board was tied to one of the gateposts by thin strands of wire and I peered curiously through the rotting gate, along the gravel path, past overgrown and overcrowded borders to see what it offered.

Whitewashed stone walls were partly hidden by a tangle of scarlet roses that surrounded a tiny latticed window over the front porch — a window with rose-sprigged curtains. My mouth felt dry and my heart began to pound again, echoing in my ears. Coldness filtered icily through me.

Rose-sprigged curtains. Pink and faded. Matching the rose-sprigged wallpaper on my bedroom wall. I could see Aunt Lucy drawing them across the little leaded-window to shut out the glaring rays of the setting sun, before she bent to kiss me goodnight and tiptoed down the creaking stairs.

Paint on the gatepost flaked beneath my fingers as they tightened; and the brightness of the scarlet roses glowed deeper and deeper against the white of the cottage walls — then a wave of darkness rushed over me.

The children's voices were shrill around me.

'Is she dead, Brown Owl?'

'Silly!'

'Brown Owl knows what to do, don't you?'

'It's the kiss of life, isn't it, Brown Owl?'

'She's only fainted, hasn't she, Brown Owl?'

'My mum used to faint before she had our baby.'

'Is that lady going to have a baby?'

Something strong and pungent prickled my nostrils making me gasp and choke at its fierceness.

One of the plump ladies held a smelling bottle under my nose, wafting it to and fro. I pushed her hand away, my eyes stinging.

The children clustered round, their faces bright with excitement.

'Does your arm hurt? Is that what made you go all funny?' one asked, her eyes wide with sympathy.

'Better now?' The plump lady sat

back on her heels, screwing the top on the small brown bottle.

'Come along now, girls. We've done our good deed for the day. You can write about it in your log books tonight when we get back to camp. Now then, are we all here?' said the other briskly.

She quickly counted the bobbing heads, smiled at me in a distracted sort of way, then hustled them off. Their voices shrilled back to us for a minute or more while we watched them weaving their way along the path to the café.

'I knew I should have taken you back to the car after we'd been to the lighthouse,' Matthew said in a worried voice. 'You're overdoing things, you know. Come on. We're going home.'

I struggled to my feet, feeling his arm tighten round my waist and lift me.

'This cottage . . . ' I said shakily, my legs trembling with exhaustion. 'I remember it, Matthew. I stayed here when I was a child. I'm quite sure of that.'

Matthew glanced back over the gate. 'You've probably been past and seen it some time. After all, you remembered seeing the Lizard Rock, so you must have visited this part of Cornwall before.'

His tone was almost disinterested as he guided me back along the track, and we slowly climbed the slope to the car park.

'But I know there's rose-sprigged wallpaper in the bedroom, Matthew,' I insisted.

'I dare say you noticed it through an open window.' He stopped and faced me, his eyes looking deep into mine. 'You're trying to go too fast. It won't do you any good and anyway, you've had quite enough for one day.'

I turned my head to read the sale board, memorising the name carefully — Trelawney & Co. Helston — and knew I had to find out more about that cottage. It was the only real clue I'd discovered so far to my past life.

5

Kati burst into my room early the next morning.

'Look!' she cried, pushing a newspaper into my hand and pointing. 'There.'

'T.V. GIRL VANISHES' I read half-way down the front page.

'It's you!'

'Me?'

I stared at the blurred picture of a sophisticated-looking girl, her hair piled on top of her head, her shoulders rising gracefully from the deep plunging neckline of an expensive evening dress.

'I'm sure it's you.' Kati's voice was uncertain now, seeing my doubt. 'Read what it says.'

'SUZANNAH EDGECUMBE (23) television producer, recently returned from filming a documentary about the starving victims of the Ethiopian famine, has been missing for four days now. Her fiancé, JONATHAN TYLER (27), T.V. cameraman, told our reporter yesterday of her disappearance.

'Suzannah would never be away for so long without getting in touch with me,' he said. 'She left our London flat for a weekend in Cornwall. A relative of hers died recently and she had some business matters to sort out down there. No one has seen her since she booked in at an hotel in Helston on Saturday afternoon. I'm frantic with worry for her safety.'

'You see. It must be you. It all fits,' Kati insisted.

Suzannah Edgecumbe.

I repeated the name over and over in my head, but it meant nothing to me.

I glanced down at the sapphire and diamond engagement ring sparkling on my finger.

Jonathan. Jonathan Tyler.

That name meant nothing either.

'Have you told Matthew?' I asked.

Kati shook her head.

'Well, if I am the missing Suzannah

Edgecumbe someone will have to be told.'

'Just fancy — you're a television producer,' marvelled Kati, her big round eyes goggling at me. 'Filming documentaries in foreign countries abroad, too.' Her face was bright with excitement as she hurried off to find Matthew.

I sat on my bed, staring down at the newspaper and then into the mirror. Tawny hair fell round my face in a tumble of heavy curls. I swept it up onto the top of my head and looked at the photo again. There was some similarity.

Matthew's face was taut when he strode into the room and almost snatched the newspaper from my hands.

'It is her, isn't it, Doctor Tregenna?' Kati insisted, peering round his shoulder. 'Shall I telephone the newspaper offices?'

'No you will not!' The words were snapped out and his blue eyes blazed furiously at her. 'No way do I want this place teeming with reporters, upsetting my patients. It will be bedlam if they do.'

'But Doctor Tregenna, Miss Edgecumbe says someone's got to be told.'

'Then I will contact the local police. They must obviously be looking for her. They'll know the right way to handle things.'

'But surely you've been in touch with them before — the day I was found?' I asked him in surprise.

Matthew turned away abruptly, ignoring my question.

★ ★ ★

The policeman sipped his coffee, put the cup carefully down on the saucer, then wiped his mouth with the back of one hand, before continuing with his questions.

'You were on a ledge, you say?'

I nodded.

'How did you get there?'

'I've already told you — I don't know. My mind's a blank. All I can remember is coming to and finding myself there.'

He looked at me in disbelief.

'You mean you remember nothing at all?'

'Nothing at all,' I answered wearily.

'Look, Sergeant, she's been asked far too many questions for one day. I can assure you my patient is suffering from amnesia — loss of memory. Isn't that enough for you? You're not helping by harassing her like this.'

Matthew glared at the man methodically writing notes in a black leather book. The policeman glanced up at him.

'Someone will have to identify her. I've contacted Jonathan Tyler. He should be here by this evening. Okay?'

He snapped the book shut and I wondered if he, too, had noticed the dismayed expression on Matthew's face at his words.

'There's nothing we can do until then. If someone did push her over that cliff like your nurse keeps insisting, then we shall have to investigate further, of course. But until I know who she is and a little more about this young lady's background, there's not a great deal of information for us to work on.'

He drained his cup and rose to his feet.

'I'll bring Mr. Tyler over as soon as he arrives, if that's all right with you, Doctor Tregenna.'

'I don't appear to have a great deal of choice, do I?' Matthew snapped.

For a moment the policeman regarded him with puzzled eyes, then left the room.

Ever since he'd seen that newspaper report Matthew had changed, becoming tense, wary, almost hostile to me. I guessed the reason. The story would get out. It had to. Then the reporters would come swarming. There was no way to stop them.

It would make a good story. Television producer mysteriously thrown over cliff. Who? What? Why? Newspapers love that kind of thing. It gives them such scope.

And it would mean disruption in the quiet, peaceful running of Tolruan Nursing Home, something that Matthew fought so desperately to achieve.

⋆　⋆　⋆

'Zannah! Darling!'

A tall fair-haired man, wearing a crumpled faded denim jacket and jeans, burst through the door and came swiftly across the room. He stopped uncertainly when I raised my head to stare blankly back at him.

'Zannah, don't you remember me? Jon?'

I scrutinised the fair hair hanging straight and thick to his shoulders, the clean-cut handsome features, the grey-blue eyes questioning mine, and shook my head.

This was the man I was engaged to. The man I loved. The man who'd placed the ring on my finger.

A stranger. A total stranger.

His mouth closed over mine possessively and I drew back, feeling his hand press hard into my back, holding me there. Over his shoulder I could see Matthew's half-shadowed face observing us and I hated the look of torment in his blue eyes.

'When can I take her home?'

Matthew hesitated before answering. I gazed imploringly at him, hoping he could read my desperate message of appeal.

'Miss Edgecumbe has been badly shocked, you realise — and of course she's suffering from amnesia. She needs rest — and quiet.'

Miss Edgecumbe. It sounded so formal. Matthew's tone was cold. Clinical and detached.

'If I take a room at an hotel nearby, she can join me there.' Jonathan Tyler's voice was determined. Quite positive. And he wasn't asking a question. This was a man used to having his own way.

'No,' replied Matthew stiffly. 'She must stay here — where I can keep an eye on her. For a while at least. Her memory may return at any time and that could be extremely traumatic for her. I must be there when it happens.'

I smiled gratefully back at him, but he regarded me without any change in his expression. He was my doctor. I was just one of the patients in his care. Nothing more. The warmth that had grown between us in such a short time was gone as if it had never existed.

'Then may I talk to her alone?' Jonathan asked impatiently. 'I want to find out what has happened over the past few days.'

'So do we all,' Matthew replied drily. 'But she mustn't be rushed. Her memory has to return, slowly and gently at its own pace. Don't try to force it. Too much haste could totally destroy her mind for ever.'

'A walk in the grounds then?' Jonathan's manner was insistent.

'Five minutes.' Matthew seemed reluctant even to grant that.

'Five minutes it shall be,' grinned Jonathan, taking my hand and leading me out into the evening sunshine.

His arm slid round my shoulders as we walked, his fingers caressing the nape of my neck and tangling in my hair. 'I love you, Zannah. Remember that,' he murmured, his lips nuzzling my ear as he bent purposefully towards me.

'Tell me about myself . . . about us,' I said, moving quickly away from him, and noticing the sudden frown that darkened his face.

'We have one of those new flats in dockland, near the Thames.'

'We live together?'

'Together?' His eyes met mine challengingly and he drew me closer to him again. 'Of course we do. We've lived there for three months, ever since we were engaged.'

He lifted my hand and turned the ring slowly on my finger, pulling me down beside him onto a white-painted seat beneath one of the flowering trees.

'Oh, Zannah, I've been so worried,' he said, leaning forward, his lips brushing my cheek and following its curve down to my throat. 'I've missed you so much.' His hands moved over my shoulders, sliding down to cup my breasts.

My body tensed at his touch, and I tried to pull away as his mouth closed over mine, his tongue thrusting deep.

'I think it's time you came indoors now, Miss Edgecumbe.'

Matthew was standing behind us, his face a mask of frozen ice, his voice brittle.

I closed my eyes, not wanting to see the remoteness in his, and walked quickly back across the smooth green lawns to my room.

'I'll see you tomorrow, Zannah.' Jonathan's husky tones followed me.

... 'Don't you worry, my treasure.' Aunt Lucy was bending over my bed, wiping away the tears. 'Hugh will change one day, just you wait and see. Poor little scrap's torn apart by the torment of his feelings. He can't trust anyone, Zannah. He loved his parents so much. Then one dies; the other goes away with someone else. Everything he loves has vanished. He's too frightened to show his feelings any more. He feels rejected, that nobody loves him at all.'

'But I want to love him, Aunt Lucy. I really do — only he just won't let me. He hates me. He keeps telling me so.'

'Just a defence, my darling. Like a shell, hiding his feelings. He's been badly hurt. Wounds like that take a long while to heal. One day he'll change though. Just you wait and see.'

I settled down under the covers while she tucked me in, feeling the brush of her lips on my brow; comforted once more ...

★   ★   ★

'Will you do something for me, Jonathan?' I asked as soon as he arrived next day.

A mischievous smile lit up his face.

'Make room for me in that bed and I'll be only too pleased,' he grinned, twitching the quilt aside.

'There's an estate agents in Helston — Trelawney & Co. Will you take me there?' I said, avoiding his roving hands.

'Anything you ask, my darling,' he replied. 'But I shall expect a thank you for doing so . . . '

He was pressing me back onto the pillows as he spoke, his body hard against mine, his eyes dark with longing as his fingers reached for the buttons on my tee-shirt.

'I want to make love to you, Zannah. Now,' he whispered huskily. 'It's been days . . . '

I struggled against him, feeling his weight forcing me down, trying desperately to twist myself away from him.

'Why, Zannah?' he asked, his eyes puzzled. 'Why have you changed?'

'I'm sorry, Jonathan.'

This man was my fiancé, my lover. We'd made love together many times before, I was sure. But to me, now, he was a stranger. His touch meant nothing, whatever it had done to me in the past. I couldn't bear the brush of his chin, rough against mine, and shrank from the familiarity of his touch on my skin. And yet, I knew, once my response must have been quite different.

'I love you, Zannah. Surely you must realise that. Nothing has changed for me.'

'But it has for me. I don't love you, Jonathan. To me you are a total stranger. How can I love you?'

It was as if I'd struck him forcibly in the face. He jerked back away from me, amazement showing in every line of his expression.

'You did once,' he said, through gritted teeth. 'And you will again.'

For a second I shivered at the ferocious intensity filling his voice.

'I'll find Tregenna and see if I can take you out of here for a while. This place quite obviously inhibits you.'

With an angry, impatient movement, Jonathan got up from the bed and strode out of the room.

'He's very passionate,' giggled Kati, coming through the door after he had gone.

'How do you . . . ? You haven't been listening, have you?' I asked angrily.

'Doctor Tregenna told me to keep an eye on you,' she retorted in defence. 'He doesn't want you getting upset.'

She bent to straighten the covers and grinned at me cheekily.

'Better than the cinema, it was. He's ever so romantic, isn't he? I wish my boyfriend was as passionate as that. How can you resist him? He'd drive me into an absolute frenzy, behaving like that, I can tell you.'

'You've got a crude mind, Kati,' I commented.

'No, I haven't,' she replied indignantly. 'That Jonathan is a turn-on for any girl. So handsome — and really sexy.'

'Oh, Kati!' I sighed, wishing I had her enthusiasm.

★ ★ ★

'An hour, no more,' announced Jonathan, returning in triumph with a satisfied smile on his face. 'He wasn't any too keen, but I bent his ear a bit, persuading him that you needed to spend some time outside these walls, if your memory stood any chance of returning.'

He slipped his denim jacket round my shoulders. 'That man is worse than a jailer, not wanting to let you out of his sight for five minutes. Does he fancy you or something? Surely that can't be very ethical. You know — doctor and patient relationship or whatever. Quite against the rules, I'm sure. Anyway, let's get moving before he has time to change his mind.'

Within minutes we were seated in Jonathan's showy red sports car, heading down the long winding drive, through the beautiful open parkland for a mile or so, until we reached the gates.

Jonathan was a fast driver and we spun round the corners at breakneck speed, passing Culdrose on our right as a helicopter rose slowly and noisily above us into the clear sky, then we turned down into Helston. Jonathan parked the car on the steep slope of the hill.

'Any idea where we find this estate agent's?' he enquired, looking up and down the street.

I shook my head. 'The 'For Sale' board only said Helston, but someone will know — it's not such a large town, is it?'

As it happened the firm was about fifty yards further on down the hill. Jonathan pushed open the heavy glass-fronted door and we went inside.

An immaculately dark-suited young man stood up to greet us with an encouraging smile.

'There's a cottage — out on the cliffs near Lizard Point,' I stated, coming straight to the point.

'Lovely spot,' enthused the man, opening a drawer and selecting a file. 'I think this would be it.' He held out a coloured photograph.

'That's it,' I replied.

'And you would like details?'

'Please,' I said eagerly.

He began to read slowly. 'It's an executors' sale — from a firm of local solicitors. The estate of Lucy Partington, deceased. In a very desirable position. Lovely sea views. It does need some modernisation and renovation, of course.'

He looked at us speculatively to see our reaction. 'She was rather an old-fashioned sort of lady, I believe, not that I ever met her. She wanted to keep the place in its original state — not a very sensible idea in this day and age.'

He smiled encouragingly again. 'Any reasonable offer will be accepted, I feel sure. It has been on the market for a while.'

'Could we go out there to have a look at it?' I questioned.

'Certainly. When would be a suitable day for you?' he said, producing a large desk diary.

'Now.'

The beam on his face clouded slightly. 'Now? I'm afraid I can't do that. My manager is out today — it's his day off. I can't leave the office — so many people call in — holidaymakers, you know. They get rather carried away with the district. Decide to retire here, that sort of thing. Unfortunately very few finally buy a property. Once they return home again, their enthusiasm usually dies.'

'Couldn't we go by ourselves?' I persuaded.

'Take the keys?' He looked rather doubtful, his eyes roving over

Jonathan's denim jeans.

'We shan't move in and become squatters,' I quickly assured him, guessing his thoughts.

'Well . . . there's nothing of value in the place so I don't suppose it would matter.'

He picked up a couple of keys, tied together with a piece of string from which a large label dangled. 'If you could return them as soon as possible, please.'

I seized them quickly before he could change his mind.

6

Lucy Partington. Could that be Aunt Lucy? I wondered as we climbed back into Jonathan's open car and returned to Lizard Point.

'Why all the fuss about this cottage, Zannah? Is it to be a holiday retreat for you and me? A nice little love-nest?' Jonathan turned his head towards mine, the wind lifting his thick fair hair and blowing it across his eyes, so that he kept brushing it impatiently away with one hand. 'Do you intend to make an offer for it, or what?'

'I just want to see inside it, Jonathan. I know I've been there before. I'm sure it could be an important clue to regaining my memory and you know how desperate I am to do that.'

The little sports car bumped over the rough grass of the car park at the top of the cliffs. It had turned into a miserable sort of day. Thin drizzle hung in the air and the sea was hidden by drifts of mist, shrouding the outline of the coast. Huddled damply in a tiny hut, an old man stretched out a cold hand to take the money as Jonathan slowed at the gateway.

'It's only about five minutes' walk. Do hurry,' I called impatiently, rushing on ahead, while Jonathan struggled to pull up the hood on the car.

'Wait for me. You'll get soaked and what will that ferocious doctor of yours do then? He'll probably banish me from his little kingdom for ever.'

I was running down the lane to find the track by the cliff-edge leading up to the cottage. Mist beaded my hair and eyelashes as I hurried through its clamminess, feeling the cold chill seep into me.

Lavender bushes hung heavily over the path leading to the front porch, scattering raindrops and sharp fragrance as we brushed swiftly past. Jonathan pushed open the door and musty air met us, heavy with dust.

I stood in the tiny hallway, looking past a small circular table, up the straight narrow stairs, then without hesitation, began to climb. At the top I turned into the room on my left, knowing already what I would find.

Rose-sprigged curtains hung at the window, even more faded now. A tall dark wooden chest-of-drawers — I knew there were five of them — stood against one wall, somehow no longer as high as I remembered.

On top was a triple mirror. Now I was tall enough to see into it, reflecting back my anxious face and the tangle of damp hair clustering round my shoulders in a frizz of wet curls. The narrow bed was stripped of covers, its mattress a faded pink to match the sun-bleached roses of the wallpaper.

This was my room.

Quickly I undid the metal pear-drop catch on the wardrobe door to stand against the back of it, pressing my hand to the top of my head as I always did as soon as I arrived, then moved away to stare at the ladder of marks recording my height over the years. My finger rested at least eighteen inches or more above the last scratched line.

A faint smell of lavender came from the shelf inside and I reached to the back of it, feeling the scrunch of brittle stalks when I drew out a tiny fragile bundle, tied with a scrap of blue satin ribbon, seeing them scatter over the floor.

'What a dump,' commented Jonathan, wrinkling up his nose as he stared round the room, a thick grey cobweb trailing down from the lampshade to brush the top of his fair head. 'But if this is what you really want . . . '

I pushed past him without answering and crossed the landing into Aunt Lucy's room, its four-poster bed still there, chintz hangings layered now with a mist of grey dust.

How many times had I curled up beside her in the warmth of crisp linen sheets, safe from the lashing fury of a gale outside, rose stems tapping the window like frantic fingers, while she soothed me back to sleep? Hugh sitting there, pale and tense, on the high-backed wooden chair beside us, wrapped in her rose-coloured eider-down, shivering panic-stricken with each clap of thunder, but refusing loudly to be a baby and join me in the comfort of her arms.

My fingers travelled lovingly down the carved bedposts, tracing their pattern, knowing each tiny acorn and smooth-edged leaf that trailed there.

Jonathan let out a strident whistle that shattered my memories with its harshness.

'What a fantastic bed,' he enthused. 'Imagine making love in that.'

I scarcely heard him. I was in the tiny room at the back of the cottage now. Hugh's room; its walls showing plain and white, despite the festoons of cobwebs and salt-covered window making it full of shadows.

Beneath the window was a low

wooden seat, acting as its sill. With trembling fingers I lifted up the lid, knowing I shouldn't. It was strictly forbidden. Hugh kept his treasures in there.

I peered down into the darkness. It could only be empty now, after all these years. Then I noticed something in one corner and slipped in my hand, my fingers closing round an object, smooth and perfect.

Tears stung my eyes as I gazed at it on my palm — a tiny curled yellow seashell — resting there as it had done oh, so long ago, held out in offering to that angry little boy.

Was it the same shell? I wondered. Had Hugh kept it after all? Going back, maybe, to search for it on the sand where he'd thrown it, once Aunt Lucy and I had gathered up the tartan rug and the scattered remains of our picnic and gone home?

'Zannah, Zannah, I love you,' whispered a voice in the shadowy darkness.

For one second I was startled,

thinking, hoping — then I realised it was only Jonathan, standing there behind me, his arms sliding purposefully round me, his lips pressing into the wildness of my hair; drawing me back to the four-poster bed in Aunt Lucy's room.

His mouth burned against mine, forcing it open; the pressure of his thighs guiding me onto the firmness of the mattress.

A prickle of sensation ran up my stomach, growing in intensity. His fingers were cool, moving gently over my breasts, teasing the nipples.

I felt my breath catch in my throat as the strength of his body slid over mine. Slowly I raised my hand to smooth the firmness of his back — and felt the seashell I still clutched press sharply into it.

With a sudden convulsive movement, I brought up my knees and Jonathan gave a cry of pain, rolling sideways away from me.

'You bitch!'

We drove back in silence to Tolruan. Steady rain was pouring down now, the lanes filled with deep puddles that splashed up over the bonnet of the little car. I could see the stark outline of Jonathan's face in the gloom, etched hard and grim.

'Will you go into Helston and return the keys?' I asked, stepping out onto the gravelled drive.

He nodded, declining to look at me.

'Later,' he answered abruptly.

Matthew Tregenna was waiting in the stone-flagged hall when we came through the door, his expression worried.

'Zannah, are you all right?' he questioned, coming forward to take both my frozen hands in his. 'You're absolutely soaked. Go straight up and have a hot bath, before you catch cold.'

'Don't order her about, she's not a child,' rasped Jonathan, giving him a furious glare.

'Miss Edgecumbe is in my care,' replied Matthew meeting his steel-grey eyes coldly. 'Taking her out and getting her half-frozen and drenched with rain is not what I recommend for my patients.'

I climbed the wide curving staircase, turning half-way up to see Jonathan's wet denim-clad back go out through the heavy oak door, then I noticed Kati quickly slip after him.

Curiously I pulled aside the curtain when I reached my room to watch the car, its hood dark with rain, gathering speed as it drove off down the driveway. A wide smile of eager excitement lit Kati's face through the rain-spattered windscreen.

★ ★ ★

. . . 'Not again, Jonathan?' I cried, glancing pointedly at the clock as he came into our bedroom.

'What do you mean — again?' His grey-blue eyes glared into mine.

'Who was she this time? That chubby little blonde in black silk or the slender dark girl with the leather mini-skirt?'

'You were the one who chose to leave the party early, Zannah, not I. I had to mingle with the other guests, didn't I? You never know exactly who you'll meet at a gathering like that. I don't want to be a cameraman for ever, you know. I've set my sights on higher things.'

'So you think some little film-set extra is going to boost your career prospects?' I scorned.

'Everyone knows someone useful in this racket — and I need contacts.'

'Not that sort of contact, Jonathan — and not quite so often.'

He slid into the bed beside me, his lean body full of determination and when his lips closed over mine, I couldn't resist . . .

★   ★   ★

'Where did you go this afternoon?' Matthew's voice was curious, as I entered the dining-room for supper later that evening.

'To Lizard Point.'

'In this weather?'

'I wanted to see that cottage again.'

Concern etched his face. 'Again? After what happened before? Oh, Zannah! How foolish of you. Were you all right? You didn't faint this time?'

'No, I was fine.'

His eyes were full of unspoken questions, his knuckles showing white and sharp as he cut into his food with fierce movements.

'It was my Aunt Lucy's cottage, Matthew. I stayed there as a child. I knew everything about it. The furniture, the curtains, even the colour of the wallpaper.'

The shell pressed hard against my hip, safe in the pocket of my jeans.

'And what else did you remember?' His eyes were burning into mine now as if trying to probe my soul.

'Nothing. I don't seem to be able to

move further ahead, only recall things from the past; my childhood. When will my mind catch up again, Matthew?' I implored.

'Soon, Zannah,' he said quietly. 'Very soon now.'

★   ★   ★

When Kati came in to talk to me next morning, there was a smug, self-satisfied look on her face.

'Was he as good as you expected?' I asked, watching her reaction.

'What do you mean?' she hedged, her fingers shaking slightly as she smoothed the bed-covers into place.

'You know exactly what I mean, Kati. Jonathan. Was he such a fantastic lover, after all?'

'How do you know what happened?' she gasped.

'It wasn't so hard to work out. I saw you getting into his car last night.'

'That doesn't mean anything,' she retorted defiantly.

'Jonathan Tyler only has one thing on his mind — permanently.'

'He said you weren't interested in him any more . . . that you wouldn't . . .' She hesitated, lowering her head.

'He's quite right, Kati. I don't care about him. He can do what he likes, with whom he likes. It doesn't matter the slightest bit to me.'

With an impulsive movement, I tugged the sapphire ring from my finger and dropped it into the drawer beside my bed, suddenly feeling free.

'You're not upsetting Miss Edgecumbe again, are you, Kati?'

Matthew Tregenna had come quietly into the room and was listening to our conversation, his thoughtful blue eyes studying my ringless hand with a strange intensity.

'Does this mean the wedding's off?' he asked.

I nodded. 'I can't marry a man I don't know.'

'And what will Mr. Jonathan Tyler have to say about that I wonder?'

'I don't really care. Why? Does it matter?'

'To him it will, I'm quite sure.' There was a quizzical expression in Matthew's eyes.

'I wouldn't want to share any man I loved,' I retorted, glancing sharply at Kati standing there, her head turned from us.

'So you do love him then?' Matthew's voice was sharp.

'No. I don't love Jonathan. I can't imagine how I ever did. I doubt that he's the kind of man who would have married me even if I had been in love with him either.'

'Is marriage that important to you, Zannah?'

'To the right man, a once-in-a-lifetime bond, never to be broken,' I replied, looking deep into his questing eyes.

I was suddenly conscious of Kati's wide stare as she listened to us, and knowing just how astute and knowing she could be, I quickly changed the subject.

'Now that I'm better, how soon do you want me to leave here? I must be taking up a room someone else needs.'

Matthew looked startled.

'Leave? Do you want to leave then?'

He paused, contemplating the idea slowly. 'I suppose there's nothing really to stop you. I'd rather like to keep an eye on you though. As I've told you before, the mind's a tricky thing. Your memory can return at any time. The knowledge of what did happen to you up there on the cliff could be a terrible shock to you, when it does.'

'So there's no need for me to be your patient any more?'

The one thing I didn't want to be was Matthew Tregenna's patient, not with the way I was beginning to feel about him.

'No, I suppose not,' he replied, pursing his lips thoughtfully. 'Apart from the amnesia and your arm, of course, you've made a perfect recovery.'

'Then could I do something useful here instead? Become one of the voluntary staff perhaps — for the time being at least. You would still have me under your observation, but I'd be doing something to help out — if you agree, that is.'

'That would be fine.'

I noticed the relief that flooded into Matthew's eyes as he spoke and wondered why.

'What can you do?' His question was blunt.

I shrugged. 'You tell me.'

'Well, we are always in need of someone just to talk to the patients. Keep them company. Write letters for them. That kind of thing. Some of them get rather lonely, cooped up in bed all day. The nurses haven't enough time . . . '

'Right then. I'll move out of here today. Is there somewhere else I can sleep?'

Matthew frowned, wrinkling up his brow in thought.

'She can share my room,' put in Kati eagerly, obviously wanting to make amends.

'Up on the top floor in the attic? I couldn't put Miss Edgecumbe up there.'

'But why ever not?' I protested. 'I've just returned from Ethiopia, don't forget. I was probably lucky to have even a blanket out there, let alone a room. Come on, Kati — show me the way.'

Kati led me to the end of the corridor where a flight of steep wooden stairs wound upwards, then up a narrower flight until we were level with the lichened rooftop. Two tiny windows looked down over the smooth, carefully tended lawns and beautiful shrub-filled gardens to the Helford River, meandering its way beyond the green of the trees.

'That bed's spare,' said Kati, pointing to a small divan. 'I'll find some covers for you.'

'Are you quite sure this is what you want, Zannah?'

Matthew, who had followed us, looked doubtfully round the plain little room and then back at me.

'Quite sure, Matthew,' I replied with a contented smile.

It was the one way I could remain near him.

7

I didn't want to see Jonathan again, not after our previous meeting, but unfortunately I couldn't avoid doing so. While I was out in the grounds with one of the elderly patients, sitting in the shade of a tall pine tree, I noticed him striding over the grass towards me. Seeing the glowering expression on his face, I knew he was in a furious mood.

Silently I raised my finger to my lips and indicated the sleeping woman, before moving away with him down one of the winding paths. From my pocket I took the sapphire and diamond ring and held it out.

'What's this supposed to mean?' he snapped, his grey eyes blazing into mine. 'Kati was burbling some stupid tale to me as I arrived.'

'It means we're no longer engaged, Jonathan,' I replied. 'How can we be? I don't love you. I don't even know you any more.'

'Don't be so ridiculous, Zannah! Your memory will come back and then everything will be just as it used to be. I love you, Zannah.'

'And what about Kati?'

'Kati! I suppose you're referring to what happened last night? So that's what the wretched girl was going on about. Now you are being stupid! As if she could mean anything to me. Kati was there — and quite obviously only too willing. What man could resist that? She's a very attractive girl, Zannah.'

He eyed me coldly for a second or two. 'And anyway you're not much use to me at the moment, are you? Even you must realise I was never cut out to be a monk.'

'Much use to you?' I stormed. 'Is that what all your protestations of love mean? I'm just someone to use in bed?'

'Oh, come on, Zannah,' he interrupted. 'You've never complained

before. Love. Sex. There's no difference.'

'To me there is,' I informed him icily,
thrusting the ring into his unwilling
fingers.

'We're engaged, Zannah. Lovingly
entwined. And I intend to keep it like
that. There's no way I'm giving you up,
so the sooner you realise that, the
better.'

Jonathan's eyes were like chips of
grey-blue steel, glinting dangerously at
me. 'It's that bloody doctor, isn't it? I've
seen the way you look at him. You're
obsessed by him. You've latched onto
him like a leech — and I suppose he's
only too eager to encourage you.'

He let his gaze roam over the
spacious grounds, the flowering shrubs
and trees, the glowing herbaceous
borders and well-kept smooth green
lawns, and on up to the beautiful old
house. Then he turned back to me with
a sneer.

'This place means everything to your
precious doctor, doesn't it? Well, it

wouldn't take much to destroy that dream. A few pictures leaked to the press. A half-hidden patch or two of mildew lurking in the operating theatre. Patients with untended bed sores. The odd maggot here and there . . . There's so much scope for a really good cameraman.'

Jonathan gave me a cool smile. 'And I am a very good cameraman, Zannah dear.'

His hands were on my shoulders now, ruthlessly forcing me backwards. I could feel the roughness of tree-bark press against my spine as his mouth bore down on mine.

'Just remember this, Zannah, I'm not going to let you go, whatever I have to resort to to keep you. You're mine — and always will be.'

His teeth were sharp against my lip as I twisted away from him, pushing the weight of my plastered arm into his face. With a cry of anger and pain, he let go of me, clutching his scratched cheek. I turned and ran back to the safety of the house, shaking with misery and fear.

'What's the matter, Zannah?'

Matthew was coming down the corridor towards me, his white coat floating round him as he moved.

I shook my head, quickly brushing away my tears before he could see them. I didn't want any trouble. I had already realised just how vindictive Jonathan Tyler could be.

'You're crying.' Matthew caught my chin in his hand and touched my cheek with one gentle finger, tracing a tear.

'It's nothing, Matthew,' I replied, turning quickly to climb the stairs.

'That Tyler fellow's been here again, hasn't he?' Matthew's eyes were suddenly blazing.

'He's gone now, Matthew,' I said swiftly. 'He won't be back. I've told him — it's all over between us.'

'But is it, Zannah?' Matthew's voice was questioning, his fingers still cupping my chin, his face close to mine.

Oh, if only it was. If only I could tell

you the truth, I thought, and hurried up the wide staircase.

* * *

'I hate him. I hate him,' Kati stormed, throwing herself down onto the narrow bed beside mine in a flood of angry tears.

'What's the matter?' I asked, struggling up through layers of sleep and switching on the bedside lamp, filling the room with a dazzle of brightness that made me blink and half-shade my eyes with one hand.

'It's that Jonathan of yours!'

'Not mine any more,' I commented drily.

Her flame-coloured lipstick was smudged over her broad lips and blue eye shadow trailed across one cheek into a messy blur.

'He's an animal!'

'Calm down, Kati,' I soothed, putting my arm round her trembling shoulders and noticing the torn neck of her skimpy cotton dress. 'Do you want to tell me what happened?'

'He tried to rape me!'

'Oh, come on now, Kati,' I chided. 'Isn't that going a bit far? After all, you have been chasing him, don't forget.'

The big brown eyes rolled round to stare at me, wild and terrified, her mouth quivering with choking sobs.

'Are you really being serious?' I asked, seeing her agitation. 'He doesn't need much encouragement, I know.'

'Well . . . ' Kati picked at the edge of the blanket with nervous fingers.

'You did encourage him?' I suggested gently.

'Maybe just a little . . . '

'And then he went too far?'

'Too far!' she shrieked. 'He went wild. There was no stopping him. He's dangerous, like a wild beast . . . And I reckon he's the one who threw you over that cliff.'

The silence of the room vibrated with

her words. I remembered the pressure of his fingers, the fury in his eyes as we stood there in the garden the previous afternoon.

Jonathan. Would he really try to kill me?

'He had a motive too,' Kati confided. 'You made joint wills when you got engaged. He told me that. You're going to be a very wealthy woman. Some aunt of yours has died. She's left you a fortune. And everything you possess will be his, eventually, he said.'

She looked up at me with wild brown eyes. 'If you'd been killed when you fell over that cliff, Jonathan Tyler would be a rich man now.'

Kati's voice was quieter now, all hysteria fading. Gently I encouraged her to go on with her tale.

'He needs money. Your Jonathan's got huge debts. He lives the high life in London, so he says. Nightclubs. Lots of parties. That sort of thing.' She eyed me strangely for a second, then continued: 'You know he snorts cocaine?'

I drew back, horrified at her words.

'He does, you know,' she said defensively.

'Are you quite sure, Kati?'

Her dark eyes flashed impatiently. 'I'm a nurse, aren't I? Of course, I'm sure. I've seen it all before. Didn't you realise — living with him like you did?'

'He was away quite a lot. Off on filming assignments for days at a time. We didn't see a lot of each other.' It was curious how I could remember that part of my life, but not others.

'Just slept together.' Her voice held a note of contempt. 'He's really vicious, you know — and desperate to get you back.'

A shiver of fear crept down my spine, as I remembered that ledge.

'You must tell Doctor Tregenna.' Kati clutched at my arm in her agitation.

'No! Whatever happens, Kati, I can't do that.'

'Why not?' Her eyes were puzzled.

'He has his own worries, without

mine to add to them.'

I regarded her thoughtfully, wondering just how far I could trust her. 'Jonathan Tyler would do anything to destroy Matthew and his life here. He's already threatened to fake pictures and sell them to every newspaper. It's not a difficult thing to do and he's a clever guy. Tolruan's in enough financial trouble without damaging smears from the press as well.'

'What can we do then?' Kati stared at me, her face full of fear and apprehension.

'Take care, Kati. Take a great deal of care.'

★ ★ ★

. . . 'Please teach me to swim, Hugh. You're so good at it. Now I'm almost ten, I should be able to swim,' I begged, standing on the edge of the seaweed-strewn shoreline, tiny waves creeping towards my toes. 'If you don't, I'll walk out into the sea and keep on *walking until I drown myself for ever.'*

'Don't be so silly, Zannah,' came Aunt Lucy's angry voice behind me. 'That's called blackmail and it's not very nice. Of course, Hugh will teach you to swim, won't you dear?' . . .

* * *

As I tossed and turned in my bed that night trying not to disturb the now sleeping Kati, my brain whirled in a turmoil of thoughts. I had to remember what had happened that day on the cliff-top. Everything seemed to hang on those few minutes. Someone had pushed me. But who?

Someone had tried to kill me. Only that tiny ledge had prevented them from succeeding. Someone wanted me dead. And whoever did it was sure to try again.

. . . *'What's the matter, my treasure?' asked Aunt Lucy, stroking my cheeks to brush away the scalding tears. 'You've been in a state ever since you arrived* yesterday. What's troubling you?'

'I'll never be able to marry Hugh,' I wailed in despair.

'Why not, my darling?'

'Because he's my cousin, Aunt Lucy. That's why. A girl at school says you can't ever marry cousins. Blood relatives, she said, can't get married. Not ever.'

'But Hugh's not your cousin, my love.'

'He must be. You're his aunt — and mine too.'

'Only by marriage,' she smiled. 'Hugh is my late husband Tom's nephew. You remember your Uncle Tom, don't you? Well, Hugh is his sister Mary's boy. No relation to me at all. Not like you are, being my own brother's child.'

I felt my heart dance with joy and relief at her words.

'Oh Aunt Lucy, Aunt Lucy, I love you so much. What would I do without you?' I cried, throwing my arms round her neck and hugging her . . .

                    ★   ★   ★

I woke next morning still feeling happy
— and then remembered Jonathan.
Would I have to go back to him? Was
that the only way to prevent him
destroying Tolruan and Matthew's life
for ever? There may be no other choice
for me. Tolruan was Matthew's life.
And I loved Matthew. I would do
anything to spare him unhappiness.

Slowly I climbed out of bed and
began to dress, seeing Kati's calm face
silhouetted against the whiteness of her
pillow, all her fears lulled away by sleep.

Swiftly I ran down the uncarpeted
stairs to the landing below where there
was a payphone and began to dial
Jonathan's number. I had to talk to
him. A girl's voice answered, blurred
with sleep, and I put the receiver down
instantly. So that was how much he
loved me!

Matthew smiled wearily from the end
of the breakfast table, where he was
pouring cornflakes into a dish as I

entered the dining-room. His face was drawn and lined, and I guessed he had sat up most of the night with one of his patients. His eyes revealed his sadness when I asked.

'Yes, she died just before five this morning, quite peacefully, in her sleep — holding my hand. I'm glad I was with her. Not that there was anything else I could do.'

'So you've only had a couple of hours' sleep yourself then?'

He raised his eyebrows ruefully.

'It happens sometimes. I can manage.'

'Oh, Matthew, you're wearing yourself out. Can't you employ someone else to help you? It's far too much for one doctor coping with so many things.'

'Good doctors cost money,' he replied simply.

'But more than half your patients here don't pay a penny. You can't run the place like that. You're not a charity, Matthew.'

Anger flared in his eyes and that

tell-tale pulse throbbed in his jaw.

'They need treatment.'

'Which you can't afford to provide for nothing,' I insisted.

'I can always re-mortgage Tolruan,' he retorted defiantly.

'But for how many times, Matthew — and for how much longer?'

It was while I was wheeling an old lady out through the wide glass doors onto the sun-filled patio and she asked about my job in television that the idea came to me.

It was so easy. Why on earth hadn't I thought of it before? If Jonathan could threaten to make bad publicity about Tolruan, why shouldn't I do exactly the opposite?

I was a television producer, wasn't I? Making documentaries. Well, I would make one about Tolruan — if Matthew Tregenna would let me. That would give fantastic publicity, just when he needed it. And, if I could do it in the right way, people might even send donations to keep the nursing-home running, although I wasn't too sure whether Matthew would approve of that.

Matthew was going to be my biggest difficulty, I realised. He was too proud to accept help from anyone, even for Tolruan. Trying to persuade him would have to be done tactfully and carefully. I had to find the right time and place to ask him.

*   *   *

. . . 'She's beautiful, Aunt Lucy. Just like a mermaid.' Hugh's voice was hushed and breathless as he gazed at me with admiring dark eyes, while I triumphantly swam towards them, my long hair trailing the water like a cloak of seaweed.

It was the first time I'd ever heard him praise me and it filled me with delight. Eagerly I lifted my arms to hug him and felt his lithe brown body twist desperately away from me.

'Oh, Hugh.' There was a note of

despair in Aunt Lucy's voice . . .

'Will you take me to the beach again this afternoon, Matthew?' I asked him. 'It must be time for you to have another day off.'

For a second he hesitated, then his wide mouth curved into a smile of pleasure.

'Why not?' he said. 'But only for an hour or so. I can't be away from Tolruan for too long.'

An hour or so might just be long enough, I decided.

I coiled my hair into a plait and twisted it round my head, pinning it there, before I stepped into the sea, very aware that Matthew was watching me, although his eyes were masked by sunglasses. I could see that tell-tale pulse beat in his cheek and wondered if he was angry in some way.

'Don't get that plaster wet, Zannah, whatever you do,' he warned.

'I'm only going to paddle,' I said, hoping that once he'd relaxed in the warmth of the sunshine and peacefulness, I could put my proposition to him without any risk of refusal. 'Come too.'

I took his hand, feeling the tension rush into it as I pulled him to his feet, but for once he didn't draw it away and I felt his fingers tighten slowly round mine as we walked over the smooth sand into the sea. Waves curled round our ankles, chilling our legs, swirls of sand rising up from between our toes to cloud the clear water.

'That's quite far enough for you, young lady. Don't go out any further.' Matthew moved away from me, suddenly diving head-first into the next rising wave and kicking out with his feet. I watched his strong tanned arms curve through the sea with hardly any effort at all, seeing the muscles ripple across his lean brown back; and I wanted him so much.

★ ★ ★

'I'm planning to make a documentary on Tolruan, Matthew,' I said, as he lay face down on the sand beside me, damp tendrils of hair drying on the back of his firm neck in the warm sunshine. 'Would you let me?'

His spine went rigid and he rolled over to look up at me, his eyes wary.

'A documentary?'

I nodded. 'That's my job, isn't it? So everyone keeps telling me. Perhaps once I get working again, it might help. Sort of therapy. Maybe jog my memory a little more?'

I reached out one finger to smooth the hair tidily into place on his neck as he bent his head in thought, expecting him to draw away, and was delighted when he didn't.

'Tolruan's such a wonderful place. All that history. It would be a marvellous story. I could trace right back to the beginning, when and why it was first built, then show what's happened from the olden times up to the present day.'

The idea was beginning to grow rapidly in my mind already, picturing just how I'd do it — the costumes, the pageantry. Enthusiasm surged through me.

'Then I could end up with the work you're doing here today. It would be wonderful publicity for you — and, of course, the televison company would pay a fee. I'd do anything to help you keep Tolruan running, Matthew.'

There was a spark of interest in his blue eyes when he turned to me, but the expression on his face remained doubtful.

'Wouldn't having a film crew there totally disrupt the place? I couldn't allow that.'

'Not necessarily. They could keep well away from the north wing where the very ill patients are. And as for the rest of them, well, it would be something for them to watch being made and enjoy. You're always saying how bored some of them get, when they're almost better again. Perhaps it would give them all an interest. Please say you'll agree, Matthew.'

He was leaning on one elbow, staring out to sea, lost in thought, as I chattered on.

'I know I could make a success of it,' I begged. 'Please let me try. I can start researching the history now, then I'll have some basis on which to present the idea to the television company.'

A slow smile crept across his face as he turned back to me, reaching out one finger to lightly brush my cheek.

'You're enchantingly beautiful when you're animated like this, Zannah,' he murmured. 'All right then. You start exploring Tolruan's history — while I consider the upheaval and think about it.'

His eyes clouded again. 'But you don't even know yet that anyone will want to make such a programme, do you?'

'Someone will, I'm quite sure of that,' I replied, full of confidence, throwing my arms round his neck, impulsively wanting to share my pleasure.

His response startled me.

The warmth of his body met mine in one long embrace, his lips burning onto mine with such passion, such intensity that I could hardly breathe for the beating of my heart; his fingers tangling in my hair, drawing me even closer to him. Then, abruptly, he drew away, his face haunted with remorse.

'I'm sorry, Zannah. I should never have done that. You're my patient. Please forgive me.'

'But I'm not your patient any more, Matthew, am I?' I laughed. 'You're forgetting I work for you now as a general skivvy and maid of all work — living up in the attic. And I doubt if it's the first time at Tolruan that the master and a maid have fallen in love.'

Happiness was bubbling through me as I spoke. Everything was so perfect — and I saw the look in Matthew's eyes as he gazed back at me, his arms drawing me close once more. Could this really be the oh so distant and remote Doctor Tregenna? I wondered.

★   ★   ★

Later, much later, I remembered Jonathan and his threats. At that moment a cloud came over the sun, hiding it, and the air took on a sudden chill. Reluctantly we climbed to our feet and shook out the thick rug we'd been lying on. Watching the sand scatter and blow away into the air, I hoped desperately it wasn't an omen for my future dreams.

8

I was impatient to make a start on the history of Tolruan as soon as we returned to the house, so went straight to the library, an enormous room leading out onto the wide terrace. Hundreds, possibly thousands, of books lined it from floor to high ceiling, mostly old with thick leather bindings tooled in gold.

Its parquet floor was polished to a high shine and bowls of flowers filled every table, their scent mingling with the smell of leather and beeswax. Motes of dust quivered on sunbeams filtering in through the huge windows and the air felt heavy with knowledge.

I wheeled a pair of wooden steps to one end of the room and climbed up them, scanning the titles until I found something I thought might be appropriate before lifting down a couple of volumes, then began to read.

As the days passed I became fascinated by the depth of Tolruan's history, while I learnt more and more about the old house and those who had lived there.

Originally it had been a small grey-granite manor house brought as part of her dowry when Katherine Burnley married Richard Callington in the fourteen hundreds.

Over the years it had grown, with the north and south wings added on to the original building. Then, in the fifteen hundreds, a tiny family chapel enclosed the remaining west side to surround a cobbled courtyard, where even now a beautiful stained-glass window still remained to commemorate the date.

The Great Hall, part of the original building, had its whitewashed walls hung with sixteenth-century armour and weapons, its enormous open fireplace laid with logs and fir cones, as if in readiness for some splendid banquet, while above the mantelpiece the faded family coat of arms was faintly discernible picked out in muted colour.

From the Hall, on one side a curved stairway led into the adjoining chapel with its barrel-vaulted ceiling emblazoned here and there with a Tudor rose.

On the far side of the Hall was the dining-room, now used daily by the more mobile patients and staff. The long polished oak table there had a history of its own, dating way back to the early sixteenth century. Every scratch and dent in it could probably tell quite a tale of long-gone days and those who had gathered round it, in good times and bad, over the decades.

Matthew had altered many of the upper rooms, dividing them into small private rooms, or larger wards, but much of their origin was still visible in the diamond-paned windows and wooden-ribbed ceilings.

A great deal of the original furniture remained in the lounge and Great Hall, most of which must be worth a fortune if anyone could persuade Matthew to sell it. Yet, it was all part of the history of Tolruan, and must remain there, never to be lost. I could understand his reason that it be so, no matter how desperate he might be for money.

I spent a long time studying the upstairs rooms. One, according to legend, had housed royalty overnight and was known as the King's Room. Some days prior to the surrender of the Royalist force at Tresillian, near Truro, on 14th March 1646, Prince Charles left Falmouth for Scilly. It was thought he may have stayed at Tolruan at that time, but in which room I could not discover.

The kitchen, despite its modern equipment, had hardly been altered at all, although now it was only half its original size, with high ceiling and a row of tiny windows near the top. The chilly stone-walled rooms adjoining it were still used for storage, despite there being several large freezers and fridges.

Much of the garden remained the

same, its trees now grown huge over the centuries, its yew hedges neat and trim, the old walls mellowed with age to a soft red brick.

Even the deep round pond was there, at one time filled with well-fed fish to be eaten during the winter months, when supplies by road were cut off by drifts of snow. Now it was thick with lilies, pink and waxen, floating in the sunshine, only disturbed by the flick of a fin from some basking golden carp or brushed by the dazzling blue of dragonflies' wings.

Spruce and larch bordered the grounds, sheltering them from the cold winds that blew across from the sea. Sitting there in the sunshine, I could easily imagine the house as it was once, filled with exquisitely dressed and elegant ladies and gentlemen, strolling the lawns beneath gossamer-light umbrellas; their carriages, drawn by high-stepping sleek horses, sweeping up the tree-lined avenue between open fields of grazing fat sheep. It was a beautiful place and already I knew exactly how I would make my film of it, filled with enchantment and delight.

In between my research I did as I had promised Matthew and helped look after his patients. Some, desperately ill, only needed the comfort of a hand in theirs. Others, bored with their long days of inactivity, wanted to talk. And always there was Matthew, often tired, often tight-lipped and anxious, but always there — and I loved him more and more as each day passed.

One of the patients, an elderly gentleman called Jim Tucker, had been a librarian locally and was proving to be invaluable by advising me where and how to find what I wanted, only too delighted to be of assistance once more.

He did a great deal of research for me, using the books and old records belonging to Tolruan. It worried me though that he was overtiring himself, but when I mentioned this, he gave me an encouraging smile.

'No, my dear, it gives me an interest,' he said, 'and makes me feel useful again, instead of just lying here. Believe it or not, my brain is still quite active. It's only my body that's rotting away.'

'Don't say that,' I pleaded.

His faded eyes smiled at me gently. 'It's true, my dear. One mustn't be stupid enough to avoid the idea. I'm growing accustomed to it now though — reluctantly.'

I clasped the frail blue-veined hands in mine and tried to hide my tears. He was so kind, so patient and understanding. Life can be so cruel. What harm had a man like this done, over the years, that he should have to suffer so terribly now?

From him I learned that one of Tolruan's past masters had owned several tin mines in Cornwall, so I needed to find out more about them. That would make the documentary of even more interest.

It was while I was in Truro, tracking down some facts about the tinners and stannery towns, that Jonathan called at Tolruan to see me again.

When I returned that afternoon, Kati met me at the door, her round eyes burning with excitement.

'They've had a tremendous row!'

'Who?' I asked, pulling off my suede jacket and brushing back my untidy hair.

'Doctor Tregenna and Jonathan Tyler.'

'Why?' I was feeling tired after the heat of the afternoon and badly needed a shower.

'About you, of course.'

'Me?'

'I was just passing Doctor Tregenna's office. I didn't mean to overhear,' Kati hastily assured me.

Not much, I thought.

'But they were shouting, so I couldn't really help it.'

'So, what did they say?' I prompted, now curious.

'He — your Jonathan — was saying

that if you were fit enough to go to Truro, you should be back in London, working again.'

'And?'

'Doctor Tregenna agreed you were quite fit but said you hadn't fully recovered your memory yet, although it was returning — gradually. You needed to be kept an eye on, he said, because the shock could upset you badly when it did return.'

Kati paused as if to see my reaction to her words, then continued:

'And he — your Jonathan — said wasn't it a possibility that you'd never remember?'

Never remember? I hadn't thought of that.

'And then Doctor Tregenna said there was always that possibility, but it was rather remote. You see,' explained Kati carefully, 'sometimes the mind blocks out things it doesn't want to remember. Usually something violent, or traumatic. It's a sort of protective device, I suppose.'

She smiled at me. 'Don't worry. It's very rare. Amnesia usually only lasts for a short time and then suddenly some slight thing acts as a trigger and everything is clear again.'

I knew already that things were slowly returning, but mainly events from way back in my past.

'Your Jonathan ended up by saying that someone from the television company was coming down to see you at the weekend.'

My heart sank. Would that mean I had to return to London?

'Maybe you could persuade whoever it is that you're working whilst you're here. After all, you are, aren't you? On Tolruan and its history,' Kati suggested hopefully.

Yes, I thought, perhaps I could.

★ ★ ★

Saturday came and with it Tom Saunders, my boss. Strangely I recognised him immediately. Ever since I'd

115

started work on the Tolruan project, that part of my mind seemed quite clear and I knew exactly what I was doing. It worried me that one part of my brain should be quite blank, yet another work in a perfectly normal manner, although Matthew assured me this frequently happened.

'Suzannah! Lovely to see you, darling,' Tom greeted, kissing me on both cheeks. 'You're looking splendid. How's the arm coming along?'

'It'll be out of plaster in a week or so now,' I replied, studying the plump, silver-haired little man with affection. 'Look, Tom, there's something I want to talk to you about. But come and see Tolruan first, then I'll tell you.'

I took his arm and led him out into the sun-drenched garden where we sat by the pond, watching the brilliant dazzle of dragonflies swoop low over the waxy-pink lilies. Carefully, I explained my idea.

Tom turned to look thoughtfully at the grey-stone building.

'It sounds great, but what about the good doctor? How does he feel about it? Jonathan says he's a difficult sort of chap.'

'Provided we can do it without upsetting the routine of the place, I think I can persuade him to agree — and, Tom, he does need the money.'

'Is that why you're doing it?' grinned Tom, patting my hand. 'You always were one to champion the underdog, weren't you?'

'Was I?' I laughed. 'Don't forget I've lost my memory.'

'Okay then, Suzannah. You set it all up and Jonathan Tyler can do the camera work.'

I felt my heart miss a beat.

'Can't I use someone else?' I asked. 'I'd prefer not to work with Jonathan.'

'Why not? He's the best guy in the business, and he's been part of your team before. You work well together.' Tom grinned at me. 'Look, Suzannah, just because your engagement's off, doesn't mean you can't co-operate together on a project. This kind of thing happens. You've just got to be adult about it.'

'I'd prefer not to have him around, Tom, that's all.'

No way did I want Jonathan and his camera anywhere near Matthew or Tolruan — I hadn't forgotten his earlier threats. Being here would give him *carte blanche* to probe around and go wherever he liked.

'It's Jonathan — or no documentary, Suzannah.' Tom was quite adamant. 'If we do it, I want the job done well and you must admit he's the best at this job, whatever your personal feelings are about him.'

Tom rose to his feet and looked quickly at his watch.

'Can't stay long. I'm flying to America tonight. There's a big deal coming off with that new serial Phil's been working on — if I can clinch it. While I'm there I could put out a feeler on this idea of yours, if you like. You know how keen the Yanks are about good old English history.' He gave a wicked grin and winked slyly. 'Try and dig up an ancestor or two if you can for them, as an enticing bit of bait. It would blend nicely into a series I've got planned for early next year.'

With a long, calculating look at the house again, he stood up. 'Think about it, Suzannah. From what you tell me, you've done all the background material. If you can film the location stuff here in four days, I could fit it into the schedule in a couple of weeks or so — before we start on this stuff of Phil's. That's going to be a lengthy one to do, so there will be no other opportunity for yours until next spring — if at all. It's now or never, Suzannah, so what d'you say?'

'Four days!' I gasped. 'That's ridiculous, Tom. Quite impossible.'

'Four days is all I can spare you. I'm doing you a favour, Suzannah. I can see your reason too. This doctor chappie is doing a wonderful job here and I can appreciate why you want to publicise him.'

He looked at me shrewdly. 'But it's four days — or not at all.'

Tom certainly knew how to get his own way, I thought angrily, then nodded reluctantly. I had no other choice.

'I knew you'd see sense. Let's go and talk money to the big white chief and see how he reacts to the idea.'

Surprisingly Matthew agreed without too much fuss once he knew I was going to be there working on it, only insisting that things were to be done unobtrusively with the minimum of disruption to the routine of the nursing-home and the patients in his care.

'That will be no trouble at all,' beamed Tom, patting Matthew's shoulder. 'Suzannah will have everything under control. She always does. You can rely on her completely. Marvellous girl. The crew can stay down in Helston. Sort out an hotel, Suzannah, will you?

I'll set about finding a suitable cast. Now let's discuss a fee.'

A look of amazement crossed Matthew's face when Tom named a figure.

'As much as that?' he gasped.

Tom's silvery eyebrows shot up and he grinned. 'You mean I could have offered less? That's our usual fee — and if it sells abroad, you'll get a repeat fee as well. That should keep the wolf from the door for a week or so, eh?'

The lines of tension and worry eased a little from Matthew's face as he signed the contract Tom had drawn up by a solicitor from Helston later that afternoon. I felt a surge of happiness fill me. At least I'd be staying on here with Matthew for a while longer.

Then, like a menacing cloud hanging over me, I remembered Jonathan and his vicious threats and realised what a problem I was going to have trying to keep an eye on him and produce the film at the same time . . .

9

How was I going to cope with Jonathan? Working with him. Unable to avoid him. I felt quite certain that his unpleasant threats weren't made lightly. He would go out of his way to prevent any success coming to Matthew — and all because of me.

With such a tight schedule, the next days were a rush of activity constantly phoning to and from London. Luckily Tom Saunders had told me to reverse the charges or I would have run Tolruan into more debt just by my telephone bills alone.

Now everything was more or less ready. Filming was to begin the next day. I knew that, if I wasn't completely organised, it was going to be even more of a frantic rush to get it done in the space of a few days. There was no margin for any error whatsoever.

Luckily the actors Tom had chosen were good and as I had decided to use the same ones throughout the history, merely changing their costume to denote the progression in time, their numbers were few. It did mean that they had to know exactly where and what they were doing though.

The personality chosen to do the voice-over commentary astounded and delighted me. If such a man didn't prove to be an incentive for viewers to watch, just to listen to that hauntingly attractive voice, then I didn't know who would. However, as he was only to do the background, there was no need to include him in the work being done on location. His voice would be added in the studio at a suitable time, after the filming had been completed.

Already I'd spent several days in London with the rest of the cast, discussing and rehearsing, before we began in earnest on site at Tolruan. The time there had exhausted me and I realised that despite my rapidly healing arm, the accident had still left a devastating effect.

I'd missed Matthew too. Oh, how I missed him. And, as my taxi stopped outside Tolruan on the day of my return, I was hoping desperately that he felt the same — and I wasn't disappointed.

His face, when I entered the stone-flagged hall, was full of welcome, his eyes delighted. Impulsively I ran to kiss him, feeling his arms tighten round my body as our lips met.

'Hullo, Zannah,' he said quietly. 'You look tired. You've not been overworking, have you? How's everything going?'

I smiled back at him. 'Everything's fine and so am I, especially now I'm back here with you again,' I affirmed. 'The cast came down with me on the train and they're staying in Helston. We're all ready for tomorrow. As soon as it's light the camera crew and trailers will arrive to get things sorted out.'

'Fine,' Matthew replied. 'I'll make sure I keep out of your way then.'

'Not too far away,' I whispered, and saw the intensity deepen in his piercing blue gaze. 'We won't want you at the start, but once we get up to the present time, then you'll be needed. After all, it is supposed to be showing the work you're doing here, Matthew,' I reminded him. 'And hopefully bring in much-needed funds.'

'I hadn't realised it was to be a commercial.' His voice was suddenly cool and distant.

'You're still not happy about it, are you, Matthew? Of course it's not a commercial,' I replied impatiently, fighting back the wave of tiredness that threatened to sweep over me. 'We want to show Tolruan and its varied history over the centuries, then lead up to the present day and all the wonderful work you're doing here. If we can promote interest in the place, that's all to the good. People will want to respond. They always do. And be honest, Matthew. You need the money.'

I'd caught a raw spot, I knew, seeing

the anger flare in his eyes, and continued quickly before he could interrupt.

'It's all very well being full of stupid pride and wanting to battle on unaided, but putting it bluntly, Matthew, you can't afford to. It costs money to do what you're doing and you've got to face that fact. Without help, Tolruan will have to close down — and you don't want that, do you?'

What am I doing? I thought — arguing with him the minute I come back, but I deeply resented the attitude he was adopting, after all the trouble I'd taken. I knew it was his dread of disrupting the life at Tolruan, but even so . . .

Matthew's shoulders slumped dejectedly as he looked at me, his eyes ringed by dark shadows.

'You're right, Zannah. I'm sorry. The last few days have been hell and I've . . . ' He stopped.

'Missed me?' I asked, needing his reassurance.

His mouth tightened slightly and that giveaway pulse throbbed in his jaw. Slowly his eyes met mine, dark, unfathomable.

'Yes, Zannah. I've missed you.' His voice was barely a whisper.

'Oh Matthew,' I cried, moving nearer, wanting his arms to close round me.

'And not just I,' he continued. 'Jim Tucker died yesterday.'

The words hit me like a deluge of icy water, cold with shock.

'Oh no!'

My dear kind friend, the elderly librarian who had done so much to help me discover Tolruan's past and make my documentary possible.

'I knew doing all that research for me was overtaxing his strength. I shouldn't have let him do it,' I raged, furious with my own stupidity.

'You gave him an extra lease of life, Zannah. He was on borrowed time. He loved those last remaining days, working with you. He really did. And there was something he wanted me to tell you. He was most insistent about it. Something about the King's Room . . . you'd be so pleased, he said. He left some notes. It turns out to be my own room.'

My tears welled over now. The King's Room. The missing part of the history. Jim Tucker had been determined to solve that mystery for me. It had become quite a challenge to both of us.

'I wanted so much for him to be in the film,' I wept.

'He will be, Zannah,' Matthew said gently, his cheek warm against mine. 'Everything he did to help you achieve it will be there, a part of him. A tribute to him.'

'I don't think I could have done it without his guidance. He was a mine of information. Oh, Matthew, if only I'd been here with him at the end.'

Matthew's fingers smoothed the tangle of hair from my eyes, wiping away my tears.

'I'm sorry, Zannah. I didn't realise he

meant quite so much to you. I should've been more gentle in telling you.'

I reached up, drawing his tired face close, and lifted my lips to his, feeling them burn against mine.

We clung there together, the air throbbing around us, never wanting to part.

★   ★   ★

I was up early next morning, waiting as the heavy vehicles trundled up the long gravelled driveway. Jonathan Tyler, fair hair sleek and shining in the sunshine, strode across the dew-wet grass towards me, lean and handsome as ever, his eyes challenging.

'How do you manage to always look so beautiful, Zannah, whatever the time of day?' he announced, taking my chin firmly between his hands and kissing me hard on the mouth, but there was no hint of affection in the action.

'I'm glad you're early, Zannah. I

wanted a run-through with you first. Locations etc., although knowing the place already, I've worked out my own ideas. Still, I suppose I'd better discuss everything with you first, so that you can agree formally.'

I frowned, hoping he wasn't going to prove difficult. It was my production and I wanted it done my way — whatever Tom Saunders had to say. Jonathan may be a brilliant cameraman, but I was determined to have the final decision on what happened.

A couple of taxis arrived a short while later and there was a surge of noise and activity as the cast emerged, led by an excited little yapping white poodle, who travelled everywhere with Barbara, our leading lady. The next hour was spent getting the cast dressed and made up, while Jonathan and I argued over the settings.

'Look, Jonathan,' I protested. 'You can't use the chapel to begin the sequence. It wasn't built until much later.'

'But it will make a fantastic opening shot,' he insisted.

'I can't help that. This is a true history of Tolruan, not some fictional fantasy. You can't alter facts. Use it later by all means, but you can't have the wedding of Katharine Burnley and Richard Callington happening there. It just wasn't built then.'

'Well, who will know that?'

'I will for one,' I replied impatiently. 'This is a documentary, Jonathan, an accurate account of what happened.'

I scribbled a list showing the date each wing was added and handed it to him.

'For goodness sake study that and plan your camera work accordingly.'

Jonathan snatched the paper from me with a furious glare and stalked away, glowering at the continuity girl who was standing nearby making notes.

'At this rate we'll never get it all finished in four days,' I sighed, then gave a groan of horror. 'Oh no, not today.'

A splendid black carriage drawn by four gleaming white horses was bowling up the drive and I hurried to tell the driver he was not due until tomorrow, when we reached the next sequence.

'Someone phoned, saying it was changed to today,' he replied emphatically. 'Tomorrow's no use anyway. We've taken a booking for a wedding down Helston way then, so it's today or not at all.'

Frantically I gathered together the cast and made rapid changes to the planned routine, while the horses stood tossing their heads, harness jingling, patiently waiting in the shade under the trees.

'But I've just spent nearly an hour getting tarted up in this wretched outfit, Suzannah,' wailed Barbara. 'It will mean changing my make-up and hairstyle completely. Oh really, you might get things right. Are you sure you're really up to all this? Jonathan tells me you're half-demented from a crack on the head or some such thing, and have totally lost your memory.'

'I'm perfectly fit, thank you, Barbara, and do put that dog elsewhere. I can't have it rushing about all over the scene,' I snapped back at her, consulting my notes to check exactly when I'd arranged for the carriage episode and feeling relieved to see that I was right. It should be tomorrow. I glanced across in time to catch Jonathan's scornful smile when he spoke to one of his crew, tapping the side of his head and raising his eyebrows as he nodded in my direction.

I could do without that kind of thing. A suspicion was already forming that he may have given the changed instructions to the carriage owner.

Luckily everything went smoothly for the rest of the morning and we hardly needed any re-takes. The carriage was only used in two sequences and by lunch-time the horses were trotting back down the drive again, leaving us to return to the planned schedule for that day.

Several of the more mobile patients and staff had been included for crowd scenes, walking in the grounds as part of a garden party during the afternoon and forming the rabble when Tolruan had been set ablaze in the late seventeenth century, which we were going to film when darkness fell.

Needless to say, the actual fire scenes would be made using models in the special effects studio at a later date, but as the twilight deepened, a feeling of excitement began to tense the air, while hurrying figures gathered on the lawn, dressed in tattered garments.

Eager, excited faces appeared when the nurses wheeled patients nearer the windows to watch the growing activity fill the courtyard and lawns, where swathes of brightness from the arc-lights illuminated the whole area.

Then the action began. Angry voices murmured, growing louder and louder into a clamour of rage; sticks and stones made of plastic and foam were aimed in fury; the pale, grubby faces of the rabble glowed in an eerie, flickering gloom, outlined by flaming brands clutched in waving fists.

'Fire the place! Let it be razed to the ground!' came the frenzied shout of their ring-leader, to end the sequence; but as he shouted out the command, a glowing brand arched through the air and in through one of the open windows, instantly setting ablaze the curtains blowing gently in the evening breeze. Flames sprang into life filling the room with flaring yellow brilliance.

'Oh my God,' I cried. 'Quick, phone for the fire brigade!' and was aware of someone running to the house, frantically trying to open doors. Each one tried was firmly locked.

'They're trapped,' a voice shrieked in terror as the smoke and flames grew.

Pale, panic-stricken faces were at the windows now, distorted with fear. Hands beat desperately at the panes of glass.

A hush had fallen on the crowd outside as they stood, gazing upward in horror, watching the fire take hold.

'Zannah!' Matthew's calm voice rang out and I saw him leaning from one of the upper windows. 'None of the fire appliances will work and the water's been turned off at the main. There's a pump and hose somewhere in the old stables. Try that using water from the pond.'

Dark figures, silhouetted against a background of arc-lights, ran towards the stables and after a minute or so began to drag out a coil of tangled hose. Someone raced with it towards the pond, while voices called out desperate instructions from either side, crowding round, making the confusion even worse.

At last a thin jet of water gushed forth, soaking those standing near it, before being directed into the burning room. There was silence, broken only by the gasping breath of two men pumping desperately in turn.

Then, in the distance, came the sound of sirens and a fire engine raced up the drive, uniformed figures darting swiftly here and there in perfect control.

'How did . . . ?' I asked as one fireman rushed past.

'Someone passing along the road saw the flames . . . telephoned at the nearest box . . . Now, keep well back.'

Under the force of their powerful hoses, the flames began to die and thick black smoke billowed forth, catching at our throats. By now a side door had been smashed and people surged in to help.

Within minutes the panic was over, the house lights came on and a confusion of voices filled the air.

Matthew caught my arm and pulled me into his office, his face sharp with anger.

'Oh Matthew, I don't know what to say,' I cried. 'Somebody obviously got carried away in the excitement. Thank God there wasn't a worse accident.'

'Accident!' roared Matthew. 'That wasn't an accident, Zannah. The phone wires had been cut so we couldn't call the fire brigade. The water was turned off at the main. All outside doors were locked and the keys removed. Every fire appliance had been tampered with so that it was completely useless and there was a pile of crumpled paper conveniently placed right under the window in that room, waiting.'

He glared furiously into my bewildered eyes. 'That fire was carefully planned and started deliberately. If it hadn't been for some passing car, this place would be an inferno by now.'

I felt the blood drain from my face.

'You think the fire was deliberate,' I gasped. 'But who on earth would do such a terrible thing, knowing that there were helpless, bedridden patients inside?'

'Anyone wanting to commit murder, Zannah.' Matthew's voice was grim. 'I didn't realise what a hazard I was taking on, by letting you stay here.'

I remembered once more finding myself on that ledge halfway down the side of the cliff. Had the person who'd thrown me there, started the fire as well?

Was it Jonathan Tyler?

But I hadn't been inside the blazing building. Jonathan knew that. He'd seen me outside all the time.

So maybe the villain wasn't Jonathan at all.

10

'Do you want me to stop the filming?' I asked Matthew, dreading his answer, as we sat drinking coffee together, later that night.

He gazed at me for a few seconds, and I knew the difficulty he must be having to decide. Then he shook his head. 'It's what you want, Zannah — and you're right, the patients are enjoying it all. It's quite a distraction, and at times they need something to divert their attention from their illness.'

'The police did say it was arson, Matthew.'

'I know, but luckily the fire didn't spread any further than that one room. If someone is trying to cause trouble then we shall have to be more cautious, but we're not going to let them win, are we, Zannah?'

He smiled into my eyes, bending to brush my cheek with his lips, before going to check his patients again.

*　*　*

Next morning all the panic had died down, almost forgotten by the thought of what was in store that day, which had the patients and staff expectantly waiting. Jonathan was already on the lawn, gathering together his crew, when I approached him.

'I'd like a word in private, Jonathan,' I said.

He turned, a confident smile lighting his face. 'Ah, Zannah, so you've realised you can't live without me then?' he teased.

'What the hell do you think you're playing at?' I demanded.

His eyebrows shot up in feigned surprise. 'You should know I never play at anything, Zannah. Everything I do is very carefully planned first.'

'Like yesterday's fire?' I questioned,

watching his face for the slightest flicker of guilt.

His smile broadened. 'Would I do a thing like that?'

'Knowing you, yes,' I replied abruptly.

'Prove it then.' His grey eyes were full of challenge as they met and held mine. 'Just because your doctor friend tries to run this place on a shoe-string, it's not surprising accidents happen. Find out when he last had those fire appliances checked. And as to careless staff leaving piles of old newspapers around, well, that's not my fault, is it?'

'So you do know exactly what happened then,' I commented, pouncing swiftly on his words.

'Who doesn't? The whole place is buzzing with tales.'

I realised I wasn't going to get very far with my questions. Jonathan was too clever to make any mistakes. As he said, he was a very careful planner.

'Oh, by the way, Zannah. I brought down a pile of post for you. It was back in the flat. Been there for days. Remind me to give it to you some time.'

I'd forgotten our flat together.

★   ★   ★

The filming that day went quickly and easily. Luck was obviously on my side. The cast Tom had chosen were all so professional that we hardly needed to do any re-takes, which are always time-consuming. By the evening I breathed a sigh of relief. Maybe, after all, I would fit everything into my allotted four days.

People were packing up ready to go back to the hotel when one of the dressers rushed up to me.

'Oh, Suzannah, have you seen Barbara's little dog anywhere? She's going frantic. It seems to have wandered off during the day, although she left it in the make-up caravan, under the trees, so it would be in the cool.'

Barbara's dog was the joy of her life. The small white poodle was beribboned and cosseted, and Barbara never went anywhere without it. She even tried, unsuccessfully, to persuade me to give the animal a small part in the documentary.

'They must have had pets, darling, even in the olden days,' she cooed. 'Everyone has pets. Weeny One would simply adore it. Do say yes, darling,' she implored.

For the next half-hour a search was carried out of every bush, every tree; then we moved into the house thinking maybe one of the patients had found the dog and taken it indoors.

By now Barbara was hysterical.

'Call the police!' she shrieked. 'Send for a helicopter! Weeny One must be found. She never wanders far from me. She worships me too much for that. It's all your fault, Suzannah. Why didn't you let me have her when we were filming? Now someone's kidnapped her. She'll be held for ransom. Everyone knows how wealthy I am.'

It was almost dark before Weeny One

was found. Jonathan came in holding a dripping bundle of bedraggled fur like a heap of discarded clothes.

'Floating in the pond,' he announced, dumping the body on Barbara's lap. 'Been there for hours, I should say.'

It took another hour and several glasses of brandy to calm Barbara. By then she was insisting on a ceremonial burial for her beloved pet.

'What else can I do with the poor little love? I can't take her home with me and bury her there. My flat has no garden. And she adored it here. Simply adored it. All those exciting things hiding in the grass for her to sniff. She must stay — even though it will break my heart to leave her.'

Matthew, who had been summoned to cope with Barbara's hysterics, gave assurance that Weeny One would be placed in the quietest part of the grounds later that night by one of the gardeners.

'Nowhere near that terrible pond,' Barbara insisted. 'I don't want my darling little Weeny One reminded of how she met her end. And you will let me have a memorial stone, won't you, darling? Nothing flamboyant, of course. Just a small tribute to a beloved companion.'

Obviously much against his will, Matthew agreed.

Throughout all this, Jonathan sat, watching with a cynical half-smile on his face, and I wondered again just how the dog had managed to escape from a closed caravan and find its way into the pond. Weeny One always went straight to Barbara, wherever she was, like a devoted sheep.

'I can't appear tomorrow, Suzannah,' she announced dramatically. 'I shall be in a state of shock and mourning.'

'But Barbara,' I pleaded. 'We need you. You're a vital part of every scene.'

'Cancel everything then,' she replied with a regal wave of her hand.

'There's not enough time to do that. We've only two days left. Filming must be finished by then. Please Barbara, don't let me down. I'm depending on you.'

'How can I?' she sobbed, dabbing at her eyes with a minute lace handkerchief. 'How could anyone, when their nearest and dearest has gone?'

'It would be the best thing for you,' Matthew assured her. 'And of course, a star like you ... so very professional ... ' He paused to make quite sure she was taking in the full effect of his words. 'With a star like you, surely the show must go on?'

I could see Barbara begin to preen, peeping at him flirtatiously over the edge of the lace handkerchief. 'Do you really think so, Doctor Tregenna?'

'You're not the kind of person to be put off your performance by anything, I'm quite positive of that,' he said, throwing me a conspiratorial glance, 'and it really would be the best thing for you to do, you know.'

'Well, if you say I should — acting as my medical adviser, of course.' Barbara turned to me graciously. 'All right,

Suzannah. I'll be there.' She gave a dramatic sigh, then continued: 'Come what may.'

As the taxis made their way down the drive into the dark starlit night, I felt my body slump with exhaustion. Matthew caught my arm.

'I hadn't realised quite what a difficult job you had, Zannah,' he smiled. 'I thought some of my patients could be awkward at times, but none so bad as that dreadful woman.'

Jonathan was getting into his car as we walked back to the front door and I saw the frown that overshadowed his handsome face when he noted Matthew's closeness.

'Don't forget to bring those letters tomorrow, will you, Jonathan?' I called out to him, interested to know who could be writing to me.

★   ★   ★

When he arrived early next morning, I was still eating breakfast in the

148

dining-room with Matthew. With a glare, Jonathan thrust a bundle of envelopes into my hand. Quickly I glanced through them and selected one with a Helston postmark.

It was from a firm of solicitors and dated several weeks before, about the time I had my accident. The contents surprised me.

Both Matthew and Jonathan stared when I gasped.

'I was right. Lucy Partington was my aunt and owned that cottage out at Lizard Point. This letter refers to my calling at the firm on the day they wrote and confirms that they are keeping the property on the market as requested.'

I folded the letter and put it back into the envelope.

'The interesting thing is that it's dated the day before I was found on that cliff ledge.'

'Isn't it about time we got on with some filming, Zannah?' Jonathan cut in abruptly, as I began to open a second envelope.

'Sorry. To be honest, I'd forgotten all about that in the excitement.'

'Most professional,' sneered Jonathan.

'You don't need me yet, do you?' Matthew enquired.

'Do we ever?' I heard Jonathan mutter under his breath.

'Tomorrow's your big day, Matthew. Today we're only up to the forties — the war years — when Tolruan was used as a military camp. We'll try not to disturb the patients too much,' I added quickly, seeing alarm rush into Matthew's blue eyes.

As I went out into the morning sunshine, a feeling of apprehension crept over me. Every day since we'd started filming something unexpected had occurred. What, I wondered, was in store for us this time? When she climbed out of the taxi, dressed from head to toe in unadorned black and clutching an enormous bunch of white lilies, Barbara's first thought was for her beloved's grave. Having located a gardener hoeing one of the borders, I asked him to take her to where Weeny One had been buried. On seeing the tiny mound of newly-turned earth, Barbara dabbed her lace handkerchief to her eyes and requested to be left alone for a while.

'Only a minute or two,' I warned her, glancing anxiously at my watch. 'You have to be in your ATS uniform ready for the first scene shortly.'

'You're so heartless, Suzannah,' she murmured theatrically, 'but never fear, I won't let you down. The show must go on, as they say, whatever anguish there may be in one's shattered heart.'

The climax of the day's work was to be an air-raid when once again Tolruan was partly destroyed. From Jim Tucker, my elderly librarian friend, I had been fortunate to discover that one of the helicopter stations on the Lizard had two war-time planes, one an old German bomber, the other a British Spitfire, and several years had been spent restoring them to their former glory. Now they were loaned out for air-displays and other special occasions.

At four o'clock both were scheduled to fly over Tolruan; the bomber to drop its dummy bombs when attacked by the Spitfire. Of course, back in the studio, a mock-up of the actual raid would be staged with models, but I was hoping we would get some semblance of action today. There could be no repeat performance. Time was running out.

By three-thirty we were all ready and waiting. The sky was a hazy blue, as it had been that day in the forties. Sheets of camouflage covered the whole building and outhouses to make them look authentic. Our eager crowd of extras wore their uniforms with pride, strolling about the grounds as they would have done in those war-time days, enjoying the sunshine.

The attack had taken everyone by surprise. One lone German bomber, limping home after an aborted raid, coming in swiftly out of the sun, flying towards the sea; the Spitfire close behind. Today was a perfect replica.

We had rehearsed everything that was to happen on the ground twice that afternoon. One take was all that would be possible in the brief time allowed, so everyone had to know exactly what they were meant to do.

Jonathan was leaning casually against the wall of the stables, smoking a cigarette, with one hand in the pocket of his denim jacket.

'Shouldn't you be with your crew over there?' I commented.

He made no attempt to move. 'There's no rush.'

'The planes could be early.'

'Don't panic, Zannah. They won't be. These things are never on time. Everything always takes far longer than anticipated.'

'Please, Jonathan,' I urged, feeling the tension rise within me.

He shrugged his shoulders, tossed the cigarette aside, and strolled across to the corner of the building.

When the bomber swooped in low, a row of mock explosions would take place, carefully wired up across the lawn to simulate machine-gun fire.

A faint humming droned through the air. Everyone tensed, ready for action. One or two looked anxiously up at the sky.

Nearer and nearer, louder and louder, then the planes were above us with a deafening roar.

The action began. Figures darted frantically here and there, racing for cover.

A column of smoke rose from behind the stables. Good, I thought, that fake bomb went well. Flames darted from the Spitfire's guns in a trail across the sky.

The bomber was almost brushing the high chimneys of Tolruan, it was flying so low.

He's cutting it a bit fine, I thought, and a prickle of fear crept down my spine. One touch was all it needed to send a chimney crashing down through the slates of the roof to where patients lay in the north wing.

A spurt of machine-gun fire hit the ground, spattering dust and gravel. The special effects crew had done a fantastic job.

Agonising screams of pain tore through the air as the plane droned slowly and heavily out of sight, the Spitfire still circling busily round it with a blaze of spluttering flame.

For a second or two more, uniformed people lay where they'd been hit, just as we rehearsed, then a murmur of voices and relieved laughter filled the air, when they began to climb to their feet, ready for a welcome cup of tea.

One remained, lying still.

Curiously everyone began to gather round him.

The man's eyes were closed in his white face, his body crumpled into an unnatural position. As we watched, blood began to ooze through the side of his trouser leg.

'Get Doctor Tregenna,' I ordered, feeling a rush of faintness spread through me.

11

'This man needs immediate surgery. The bullet will have to be removed as quickly as possible.' Matthew was grim-faced as he stood up, wiping blood from his hands. 'Do you always use the real thing?'

'Real thing?' I questioned, puzzled. 'What do you mean? It can't be a real bullet, Matthew. Everything's faked. That was set up — it's like a string of firecrackers that are triggered to go off at a given moment.'

'Try telling him that,' Matthew replied tersely, snapping shut his bag. 'He's been shot at quite close range. I'm sorry, Zannah, but the man has a bullet in his leg and he's losing a lot of blood. The quicker I operate, the better.'

'It's a jinx,' murmured Barbara, looking round nervously. 'Is the place haunted, Suzannah? There's something very evil going on here. First that terrible fire, then my poor darling Weeny One, now attempted murder. Thank goodness tomorrow's our last day. I shall be only too grateful to reach home again unscathed. It's been a disaster right from the start. What a relief it wasn't one of us — just an extra. I suppose the poor man's insured. Really you don't expect to be wounded by a war-time bullet in this day and age, do you?'

I felt terrible. Despite assuring Matthew that Tolruan would not be disrupted, it had been. Fire engines. Police. And now this. More police arrived about ten minutes later. Then the questions began. Who was where, and when? What were they doing?

'Jinxed, ever since we arrived,' I could hear Barbara's voice, shrill and excited, above all the others.

No gun was found though.

* * *

It was late in the evening before I saw Matthew again. He looked drawn and tired.

'How is he?' I asked.

'Fine now this is out.' A bullet rested on his outstretched hand. 'I'm just on my way to give it to the police inspector.'

'But how on earth did it happen?' I asked.

'From the angle the bullet entered his leg, it was fired from above and slightly from the left.'

I remembered that Jonathan and his camera crew had been standing to the left of where the man had fallen. Surely it was impossible for him to shoot a man right there in front of everyone? But all eyes had been looking upwards, watching the two planes. And Jonathan, with a gun his pocket, could have fired through it, not caring who or where he hit.

'I'm sorry, Matthew. It's all my fault.'

'You weren't to know what was going to happen, Zannah, but I wish to God

I'd never agreed to all this,' he bit out angrily. 'All I was worried about was upsetting the routine . . . I never imagined there'd be a maniac loose in our midst.'

He reached out to touch my hand and gave a rueful grin. 'But, to be honest, I have to admit that it's given everyone some excitement. I've never known the morale of Tolruan to be so high! No one can wait to see what's going to happen next. Half the patients are Miss Marple and the rest are Sherlock Holmes, working out their theories. None of them has any time to feel ill.'

'Well, I'm glad you can see the funny side,' I commented wryly.

'Tomorrow's my big day then, Zannah?'

'Yes,' I replied. 'Tomorrow's your big day.'

My stomach churned at the thought of the scenes inside the nursing-home — showing Matthew and his work there. Knowing just how much hatred

Jonathan felt towards him, I was terrified of what would happen.

That night I hardly slept at all, tossing and turning, my mind filled with visions of the plane, low and heavy in the sky, droning overhead, then the spurt of gunfire sending up dust and smoke from the ground. I tried to picture exactly what Jonathan had been doing at the time, but my eyes too had been fixed on the plane.

Whatever else happened, I knew I had to keep a very close watch on Jonathan Tyler all the time we were filming inside Tolruan.

* * *

Misty rain was falling when I pulled back my curtains next morning and saw the garden overhung with grey dampness. Kati slept, one arm flung over the covers, her face beautiful in its composure. Quickly I dressed and made my way downstairs to check once more the routine I had organised for the day.

Everything had to be done as quietly and unobtrusively as possible. I knew Matthew would never forgive me if I upset his patients again and today we would be in direct contact with them.

Whether it was the fact that policemen were still at Tolruan, continuing their questions, or because Jonathan was under constant supervision as his camera crew followed Matthew's progress during an average day, I don't know but to my relief everything went quite smoothly. No mishaps at all. Maybe even Jonathan was moved to compassion by the care and devotion Matthew and his staff showed for the desperately ill and dying.

Once all the equipment was packed into the vans ready to go back to London that evening, I went to find Jonathan.

'Thank you,' I said and saw the undisguised surprise in his eyes.

'What for?'

'Not staging anything unpleasant today.'

'Why are you so positive it's me, Zannah?'

'Who else would want this project to fail, Jonathan?' I asked. 'Who else hates Matthew and all he's trying to achieve at Tolruan?'

'Has it occurred to you, Zannah, that maybe someone else caused those unpleasant events? And only today, when the cameras were on him all the time, was he unable to carry out another one?'

I felt my heart miss a beat at the obvious meaning of his words.

Matthew.

Jonathan was hinting that Matthew Tregenna had caused the accidents.

'You'll be coming up to London to sort out the rest of this thing, I suppose, Zannah?'

I nodded, my mind still turning over his malicious words.

'Well, don't forget we have our flat there. Why stay in an hotel when your own bed is waiting for you?' He gave a half smile. 'Oh, don't worry, Zannah. I shall be in America, filming that serial of Phil's. Tom Saunders insisted I do it. It's a fantastic opportunity. Who knows what contacts I'll be able to make over there.'

He handed me a key, then reached out to cup my chin and drew my face towards his. I waited tensely for his mouth to take mine, but he just gazed down at me, a strange look in his eyes.

'Can you really be so sure I'm the villain, Zannah? Would I risk ruining my chances, when I've such a future ahead of me?'

He picked up one of the camera cases and swung it over his shoulder. 'There's a party at the hotel to celebrate later. You must be there. After all it is your production, isn't it?'

'Not tonight, Jonathan,' I answered, feeling exhaustion drain into me. 'Don't forget I'm still convalescent, so it's early to bed for me at the moment.'

'That must be very convenient for a certain person, I dare say,' he said meaningly, nodding his head in the direction of Tolruan, and climbed into the van.

★   ★   ★

'What did you think of it all, Matthew?' I asked, going into his office once the excitement was over and everyone had left.

'I'm afraid it's not my kind of life, Zannah,' he said, pushing a weary hand through his thick dark hair.

'I'm not sure it's my kind of life either any more.'

His eyes widened slightly. 'What do you mean?'

'Oh, I don't know. It's just that . . . since I've been here in Cornwall, London life doesn't have quite the same appeal — or perhaps I've changed. That bang on the head did something maybe!' I said lightly. 'Anyway, I've decided to buy Aunt Lucy's cottage.'

I expected some reaction from Matthew, but he remained silent, just gazing at me with those deep unfath-omable blue eyes as if he couldn't quite understand. Did I have to spell it out to him? Tell him I loved him? That I wanted to remain here in Cornwall with him for ever? Couldn't he realise how I felt?

'I didn't mention it at the time but one of the other letters Jonathan brought me was an acceptance of a play I'd written for television,' I said. 'I've been thinking about giving up the production side and taking up writing instead. Aunt Lucy's cottage would be ideal. Remote. Peaceful.'

And near to you, I wanted to add.

Matthew laughed. 'Remote and peaceful! Just wait until you've seen it in a gale, waves thundering right up the cliffs, rain lashing against the windows. You might regret it then.'

He raised his eyes to mine and said softly, 'But I'm glad you're staying, Zannah. Very glad.'

★ ★ ★

165

Now the location side of the filming was finished, I decided I must visit the solicitors in Helston and try to find out exactly what was happening about Aunt Lucy's estate.

'Miss Edgecumbe,' I announced to the receptionist. 'I have an appointment with Mr. Danvers.'

After waiting for a couple of minutes, I was ushered into a large book-lined room and greeted by an elderly white-haired gentleman.

'Miss Edgecumbe, how nice to see you again.'

'Again?' I stared at him, puzzled.

'Yes, don't you remember? You called to see me with the other beneficiary Hugh Taylor, oh let me see . . . it must be about six or seven weeks ago now. Soon after your aunt, Mrs. Partington, died. I wrote to you both confirming your instructions to us. You did receive my letter, I hope?'

Of course, I realised. That was the reason why I'd come down to Helston — to visit the solicitor — just before my accident. Quickly, I brought him up-to-date with what had happened since then.

'Yes, I gathered there had been some unfortunate disaster. It explains why I heard nothing more from you. I'm so sorry. You're fully recovered now, I hope?'

'Not quite,' I replied. 'Part of my memory is still rather vague — including just how the accident occurred. Perhaps you could tell me exactly what happened the day I came here?'

'Of course, my dear. Would you like some coffee?' He buzzed through on his intercom. 'Two coffees please, Miss Treloar.'

As we sat drinking them, he told me about my aunt.

'Mrs. Partington consulted us infrequently, although she was a client of ours for a good many years. Small matters used to crop up and she would ask our advice, but she was always rather careful with her money and regarded solicitors' fees as somewhat excessive and unnecessary.' He smiled slightly, as if it were a joke.

'We did persuade her to let us draw up her will though. Tricky things, wills — so easy to write, people think, but full of pitfalls if worded incorrectly. She was very ill at the time, you know — and it can cause an awful lot of complications if a person dies intestate. More coffee, my dear?'

I shook my head, eager to learn more. 'The cottage,' I questioned. 'Why is it on the market? Surely it should become part of her residuary estate?'

'Mrs. Partington put it on the market herself, just before she went into hospital for the last time. I visited her there to take her instructions. She was in a very poor state by then. 'Sell it, Mr. Danvers,' she said. 'And put the money into my estate for when I'm gone.' As you know, she had made her will leaving everything to be divided equally between yourself and Hugh Taylor, her husband's nephew. You and Mr. Taylor both agreed to continue with the sale, after her death.'

'But the cottage hasn't been sold?'

'No,' he replied cautiously. 'It needs a lot of renovation, I gather. And of course, its position is rather remote. Very exposed to the elements, and quite cut off in the winter at times. There was some interest for a short while early on, but unfortunately that soon ceased.'

'Could I buy it?'

'You, Miss Edgecumbe?' His voice was surprised.

'Yes. I've decided to give up my work in London,' I explained. 'Since my accident, well . . . things have changed slightly. I've decided to write for television instead. After all, I've worked as a producer for long enough to know the kind of thing that's required. Down here, in the peace and quiet, I'm sure I could do something. And, if it doesn't turn out to be profitable, then I can always go back to working in London again.'

'You mean, you wish to buy out

Hugh Taylor's half-share in the property?' Mr. Danvers mused thoughtfully. 'We shall have to contact him, of course, to get his instructions.'

'Don't worry. I'm quite happy to wait and do it all properly, but could I rent the cottage in the meantime, until everything is sorted out? I'd like to move in by the end of the month.'

Mr. Danvers looked worried. 'Move in? Well, I suppose you do own half of it, as a beneficiary in Mrs. Partington's estate. I shall have to consult my partner on the legal side of that. The end of the month, you say? That's only a fortnight away, Miss Edgecumbe, but I'm sure we can let you know before then.'

Mr. Danvers rose and held out his hand.

I spent most of the next couple of weeks in London tidying up things to do with my job and making sure the documentary on Tolruan was completed. It would not go out on screen for months yet — maybe mid-winter or early spring — but everything had to be ready.

The one thing that worried me most was sorting out all the belongings I still had in the flat, but as Jonathan was to be in America filming, I decided to stay there for the middle weekend and do all that was necessary then.

I ate out and arrived soon after eight o'clock, deciding I could start packing some of my clothes that evening.

It was a beautiful flat. I'd quite forgotten just how magnificent it was. Expensive and exquisitely furnished. Did I or Jonathan own it? I wondered.

My clothes surprised me, seeing them hanging, polythene-wrapped, in the long glass-fronted wardrobe. Row after row of silk, satin, cashmere and wool. I was apparently a sophisticated and well-dressed lady about town. Strange that now I had become quite countrified in my dress, happy to go around in jeans and tee-shirts. But then, living in the wilds of Cornwall in future, I wouldn't need sophisticated clothes any more.

Should I pack them or leave them? Selecting a few less flamboyant garments, I put them in my case to take with me. Then, tired by a week of activity at the studio, I decided to have a shower and go to bed.

The bathroom was quite exotic with a deep jacuzzi bath, big enough for two, and matching jet-black washbasin and bidet. Soft thick white carpet covered the floor.

I saw myself a dozen times at least, reflected in the mirrored glass of the walls whilst I quickly undressed and pinned my long hair on top of my head, before feeling the soothing warm spray of the shower stream over me.

Fragrant clouds of powder floated round me as I dusted myself dry with a huge swansdown puff, then felt the coolness of silk slide over my body when I slipped on one of the nightdresses I'd found in a drawer.

It was after midnight when I fell asleep, deep in the wide king-size bed that once I'd shared with Jonathan. Ivory silk sheets covered it and soft subdued lighting was hidden in alcoves, subtly illuminating the pale walls.

★   ★   ★

A rustle of movement woke me. Someone was in the room. I could hear the faint sound of breathing.

Tensely, I lay there, wondering what I should do. The phone was by the bed but if I made a move towards it, whoever was there would hear me and what would happen then, I dreaded to think.

It must be a burglar, thinking the place was empty.

Cautiously I stretched out my hand towards the phone — and felt it seized in strong firm fingers.

A sudden glow of light filled the room and I found myself gazing, terrified, into a face I knew only too well.

'Jonathan!'

'My darling Suzannah! So you just

couldn't keep away from me after all,' he drawled, still gripping my wrist.

'But I thought you were in America,' I cried, trying to pull my hand away.

'Postponed for a week — Phil's gone down with flu. But that's not very flattering, is it? Aren't you pleased to see me? Surely all those weeks away from me must be producing withdrawal symptoms by now?'

His fingers were caressing my hair as he spoke, his eyes dark with longing as they gazed down at me.

'This one always was my favourite nightdress,' he smiled, sliding it off my shoulders, his lips burning against my skin.

I clutched desperately at the bedcovers, struggling to move away from him, but he was far too strong.

'Oh, Zannah,' he murmured huskily. 'I've missed you so very much.'

I felt the stubble on his chin sear against my cheek when his mouth crushed down onto mine, forcing the breath from my body.

And then the door bell rang, echoing hollowly through the pulsating darkness, strident and loud.

Jonathan ignored it, his hands sliding over my breasts, cupping them roughly.

The bell continued to ring.

Furiously Jonathan rolled away from me and I ran towards the door, opening it wide.

Matthew stood there, his eyes full of welcome — a welcome that changed to a look of surprise as he stared at me, my hair cascading in a confused tangle round my bare shoulders, the torn black silk of my nightdress clasped to my body.

'Zannah!'

I seized his hand and pulled him into the room, throwing myself into his arms.

'Oh, Matthew!'

'I'm sorry — did I wake you? I came up to London to interview someone as a future partner for the nursing-home. You've been suggesting it for ages now, haven't you? It took me some time, but at last I realised you are right. I do need help. And knowing you were staying here this weekend — I had to see you, Zannah.'

His hands were either side of my face now, drawing it towards him, but before I could speak there was a movement in the bedroom doorway and Jonathan stood, leaning against it, a towel draped round his naked body.

'Why, Doctor Tregenna,' he drawled. 'How nice to see you. Come now, Zannah. Offer the doctor a drink. He's obviously made a long journey to visit us, darling.'

I saw the expression in Matthew's eyes — stunned, shocked; then furious as he turned to me, his face bitter.

'My apologies, Miss Edgecumbe. I had no idea you had returned to your lover. How very stupid of me. I see now why you were so very eager to come back to London.'

He opened the door savagely, then, giving me one long contemptuous look, went out.

'Matthew!' I cried. 'Please listen to me . . .' But the door slammed shut behind him.

'Dear me, Miss Edgecumbe,' mimicked Jonathan. 'I do believe you've upset the poor doctor.'

'How could you!' I stormed, beating my fists furiously against his bare chest.

'Quite easily, my darling Zannah,' he laughed, seizing my hands in his and holding them firmly. 'Didn't I warn you that you were mine and I had no intention of letting you go? Now perhaps you'll believe me.'

'I hate you!' I raged.

'Do you?' he challenged, pulling me so close that I could feel the pounding of his heart like thunder against my skin.

Furiously I tore myself away, seized my clothes and ran into the bathroom, locking the door.

My pale tear-streaked face surrounded me in the mirrored walls. Matthew was gone. And having seen us together like that, how could I ever persuade him that Jonathan meant nothing to me any more?

Dressing quickly, I went back into the bedroom, picked up my case and walked to the front door. The sooner I returned to Cornwall, the better. I had to see Matthew and convince him of the truth.

Jonathan lay on the bed, hands clasped behind his head, watching my departure with a mocking smile on his lips.

But when I reached Tolruan, Matthew refused to see me at all, let alone listen to my explanation.

12

I had telephoned Mr. Danvers, the solicitor, while I was in London and discovered that, although he'd been unable to contact Hugh Taylor at the address given to them, he and his partner had decided in the circumstances to let me reside in the property for the time being.

'With the winter coming on, Miss Edgecumbe, the cottage should be looked after. I am sure Mr. Taylor will not object. He seemed a reasonable young man, if somewhat quiet and withdrawn. We will continue trying to locate him, of course, but every letter so far has been returned from the address he gave us marked Gone Away.'

With Matthew showing only coldness towards me, I decided the sooner I moved out of Tolruan, the better. Whatever I tried to do, Matthew made it quite clear that he wished to have nothing to do with me, going out of his way to avoid even seeing or meeting me. On the rare occasions when we did, he was so abrupt I could have wept.

'Won't you let me explain, Matthew?' I pleaded as I stood in the beautiful Great Hall waiting for a taxi to take me and my belongings to Aunt Lucy's cottage.

'What is there to explain, Zannah? You live the way you wish. It's nothing to do with me.'

'Isn't it, Matthew?' I asked.

His face flushed slightly and the revealing pulse flickered in his cheek, but abruptly he turned on his heel.

'I hope you settle in comfortably,' he said in a bleak tone. 'Contact me if you need anything.'

So formal. So distant.

'I'll try not to bother you again, Matthew,' I replied, feeling the tears burn in my eyes.

★ ★ ★

The taxi driver helped me carry my cases along the track to the cottage.

'Oh, m'dear,' he gasped breathlessly. ' 'Tis a bit far out, isn't it?'

I pushed my way up the overgrown path, stepping over the straggling lavender bushes, smelling their pungent fragrance as they brushed against my clothes. When I opened the front door, a feeling of welcome surged towards me. It was as if Aunt Lucy and her love still filled the cottage.

After paying the taxi driver, I stood there, looking round. Dust and cobwebs covered every surface. Damp had darkened the walls in patches near the ceiling. The curtains hung, bleached pale and thin, at the salt-caked windows. A rush of dismay suddenly flooded over me. Why had I come here?

Then, as I gazed down at the view stretching far away into the distance, the crinkled grey-blue of the sea flecked with white horses, the dark, stark serpentine cliffs, the thick tussocky grass blowing in the wind, I knew. This was my home. This was where I had to be, here.

It was a month before I could begin to write. First the whole cottage needed cleaning from top to bottom, walls and windows painted, new curtains sewn. I tried to keep everything as Aunt Lucy had made it, even down to the rose-sprigged curtains in my room, searching the shops in Helston, Penzance and Truro before finding the same material again.

It was still my room, looking out over the tangled shrubs in the now hidden borders and waist-high grass where once had been a tidy lawn edging the weed-choked lily pond. Everything had been so neglected in the past years, but one day I'd restore the garden to how I remembered it when I stayed there as a child.

Matthew didn't make any attempt to see me. I wondered where he went now for his afternoons off, or maybe he didn't bother with them any more. Sometimes, looking out at the sea, I'd feel my heart miss a beat as a tall dark figure ran down the beach and began to swim with strong, firm strokes — but it was never Matthew.

Autumn had come and gone, the occasional yellowed leaf was still left clinging to an apple tree bent low, away from the sea. The days grew shorter and shorter, brilliant sunsets flaming the evening sky with such glorious colour I wished I could paint. I walked for miles, feeling the wind cold on my skin, breathing in its saltiness, remembering. I remembered so much now that I was here. Each day it was as if a page turned and I was back in the safety of Aunty Lucy's love — with Hugh.

* * *

... 'He's not coming this year, my darling. Too old for the seaside, so his mother says. They're going to Switzerland or somewhere. Educational. Hugh will be going to university in October. I *can hardly believe he's nearly a grown man. Seems only like yesterday we were all down here paddling in the sea.'*

'Won't he ever come back here again?' I asked wistfully, feeling as if my heart would break.

'Maybe, my pretty one. One day . . .'

★   ★   ★

Did he ever come back here? I wondered, gazing round his room. I'd whitewashed the plain walls, and re-painted the window frames but apart from that, left it exactly as it was. One day, I hoped, he might return.

My memory was nearly complete. Only one missing piece remained. That night. The night on the cliff ledge. And how I'd got there. No matter how much I tried, that one vital part of my mind was hidden, cloaked in mystery.

Kati was a frequent visitor. Almost too frequent.

It was from her that I learned about Matthew's new partner at Tolruan.

'Doctor Svensen. She's really beautiful,' Kati enthused. 'Scandinavian, I think.
Tall, blonde, with a fantastic figure.'

Why did I feel jealous? It wasn't my
concern. Matthew had made it quite
plain that he was not interested in me
any more. Besides, she was his working
partner — and I comforted myself that
Matthew was a firm believer in moral
ethics.

'She really fancies Doctor Tregenna,'
Kati continued. 'Anyone can see that.'

My heart sank.

And what about Matthew? Does he
fancy her? I wondered.

'You must come to the Christmas
lunch, Zannah. We're each allowed to
bring an outside friend. Doctor Svensen
says it will do the patients good to meet
strangers.'

Strangers. Was I now a stranger?

'That's very kind of you, Kati, but I
shall spend the day here. It will be my
first Christmas in the cottage.'

'But you can't do that! Not Christmas. Not on your own.'

185

'I prefer it that way, Kati,' I said firmly.

Of course if Matthew asked me, it might be different.

Three days before Christmas I received a formal printed card bordered with tiny sprays of holly.

HELGA SVENSEN AND MATTHEW TREGENNA REQUEST THE PLEASURE OF YOUR COMPANY FOR CHRISTMAS LUNCH AT TOLRUAN —
12.00 noon.

Scrawled in thick black ink were the words — Please come, Zannah.

I couldn't refuse.

Rummaging through my wardrobe I searched for my most glamorous dress — one I'd brought down from London with me — black lace, with a close-fitted bodice and full-gathered skirt, far too sophisticated for everyday Cornish life, but suddenly I wanted to be noticed, wanted to stand out. I had yet to meet the beautiful Doctor Svensen.

The same taxi driver collected me, struggling up the path, his thinning hair blown over his red-cheeked face, his collar turned up against the wind.

'I never thought you'd last out here, m'dear. Taken bets, I would, that you'd be gone by now,' he grinned, slapping his hands against his sides to warm them. 'London lady like you.'

Tolruan looked magnificent, its grey stone set against a background of frost-covered trees, sparkling in the sunshine, the wide lawns gleaming white. A typical Christmas card scene.

Kati welcomed me. 'Oh, Zannah, what a lovely dress! I'm so glad you came. It took me ages to persuade Doctor Tregenna to send you an invitation. He seemed to think you'd be away in London or something.'

My heart sank with disappointment. I had hoped it was Matthew's own idea.

There were still a few patients there that I recognised and they greeted me with warmth, commenting on my long absence. I was surrounded by a group of them, all chattering at once, when I became aware of Matthew's intense blue eyes surveying me across the room. It was several weeks since I'd seen him, but even so my heart began to pound and I felt my cheeks burn under his silent stare.

Beside him stood Doctor Svensen. It could only be Doctor Svensen. Kati was always very descriptive, but this time she had understated the lady's appearance.

Helga Svensen was more than beautiful. Her looks were quite devastating. Pale, almost silver hair was coiled on top of her head in a thick shining plait. Her skin was smooth and golden; her features delicately carved like those of a statue. Her eyes, green like a cat's, were turned towards me. They flared with instant antagonism. A mutual feeling.

I felt my back stiffen as I looked at her, seeing her hand slip through Matthew's arm in a swift possessive movement.

'Zannah!' Matthew's voice was warm,

revealing for a brief second all the old welcome, then his face became remote again. 'This is Helga, my new partner.'

Her hand was ice-cold as it brushed mine, her eyes the same.

'I have heard about you — the amnesia case?' Her accent was softly attractive.

I nodded. 'I'm quite recovered now.'

'Are you?' Matthew's eyes showed interest.

'Oh, a few bits of my memory are still missing. The final part — how and why I fell,' I said lightly.

'You're looking well.' The clinical detachment was back. Matthew regarded me as an ex-patient, nothing more. 'How's the writing?'

'Progressing. It should do. I work at it all day and every day. There's not a lot to do on the Lizard at this time of year — and not many people visit me,' I said pointedly.

'It takes a while to become part of the community,' answered Matthew, refusing to meet the challenge. 'Now, shall we go in to lunch?'

The long table shone with a high polish and gleaming silver. Scarlet napkins and brightly coloured crackers decorated the side plates. A bowl of berried holly and poinsettia stood in the centre. As the more mobile patients came in, gasping with delight, an air of excitement began to fill the whole room.

Matthew sat at the head with Helga on his right. I sat facing her, feeling her antagonism spike its way across the table towards me.

'When do we see the documentary, Zannah?' Matthew asked politely, obviously making conversation.

'Around Easter, I believe. It's completed now. I was in London a couple of weeks ago, seeing a run-through. It's good, Matthew. I think you'll be pleased.'

'In London?' There was a sharpening of his voice. 'And how was Jonathan Tyler?'

'I have no idea,' I replied coldly. 'I didn't see him.'

Matthew's eyes questioned mine.

'Ah yes,' commented Helga. 'Your handsome lover — Kati has told me all about him.'

Kati would, I thought crossly.

'We were once engaged,' I replied. 'Before my accident. Not any more though.'

'But lovers still, I dare say?'

'No,' I snapped.

She smiled, a thin smile that didn't reach her eyes, glancing sideways at Matthew as she did so, fully aware of the tiny tell-tale pulse of anger beating in his cheek.

'Your cottage is remote? Not many people visit, you say? A good place to entertain a lover?'

Why did I let her upset me? It plainly gave her much pleasure.

'I haven't seen Jonathan Tyler since I went to London just before I moved into the cottage,' I retorted, mainly for Matthew's ears. 'And I don't wish to either.'

Helga smiled, having done as she intended — annoyed me and revived

Matthew's resentment. The rest of the day was spoilt.

It was a pity. Everyone had worked so hard. The lunch was delicious — clear soup or tangy prawn cocktail, roast turkey with all the trimmings, Christmas pudding so dark and rich with fruit, it was difficult to put a spoon into, mince pies with fairy-light pastry that melted in your mouth, thick clotted Cornish cream, and a selection of cheese to end the meal — for those with enough room.

In the afternoon some of the nurses performed a nativity play with Kati a solemn dark-eyed Mary, then after tea we sang carols by candlelight, all sitting in the Great Hall where a huge log fire blazed in the grate.

I wondered how many ghosts from the past joined us, re-living their Christmas of long gone, still celebrated in the same way despite the passing centuries.

It should have been a delightful day, but somehow, seeing Helga so close to

Matthew, one hand resting along the back of his chair, her fingers occasionally touching his dark hair, distressed me. If this was how she behaved in a group of people, what was she like when they were alone?

I knew I shouldn't care. But I did.

'I'll drive you home.' It was a statement not a question as Matthew slipped my coat round my shoulders.

'There's no need. I ordered a taxi.'

'And I cancelled it when it arrived a few moments ago.'

Silently I climbed into the front seat and waited for him to start the engine.

'I'm sorry if the day was a disaster for you,' Matthew said as we travelled slowly down the long drive.

So he had noticed.

'It was kind of you to ask me,' I replied stiffly.

'Oh Zannah, do we have to be like this?' he implored, suddenly jolting the car to a halt and taking me by the shoulders.

'It was not my choice, Matthew. You

wouldn't see me or even listen to me. I tried so hard to explain to you. I thought Jonathan was in America that night when you found us together. He should have been.'

I reached out to touch his cold fingers as they gripped the steering wheel. 'I left as soon as you'd gone. Please believe me, Matthew. Jonathan means nothing to me.'

Slowly and gently his lips caressed my cheek, moving lightly across it until they reached my mouth.

A whisper of snow brushed the window, patterning it with a dapple of whiteness.

'I'd better get you back to your cottage before it settles and we get cut off.'

I smiled contentedly, in the closeness of his arms. 'Would that matter?'

'I wouldn't mind, but my patients might.'

'You're far too dedicated, Matthew. I almost feel jealous of Tolruan at times. Surely, now you have Doctor Svensen to assist you, things must be easier.'

'They are, but Tolruan will always be my first responsibility, Zannah. You must understand that.'

'I do, Matthew and that's why I love you so much. You're such a devoted and caring man.'

The car crunched down the lane and stopped. Matthew helped me out, leading me along the track, the snow thickening fast now, whirling round our faces, covering our hair with melting flakes, chilling our skin.

He pushed open the gate and we walked up the path, the lavender bushes sparkling with rime in the moonlit darkness. Quickly I opened the door and Matthew's arms closed round me, his face icy cold against mine.

'Zannah darling! What an age you've been,' drawled a familiar voice.

I felt Matthew pull away, his body stiffening, his eyes turning to meet mine with a look of disgust as Jonathan Tyler came down the stairs.

'Matthew . . . ' I whispered, but it

was already too late. Matthew was striding back down the snow-hidden path towards the gate.

'Merry Christmas, Zannah,' chuckled Jonathan. 'It seems that once again we've upset the dear doctor.'

'How did you get in?' I demanded, throwing my wet coat on the chair.

'Don't you remember, in the summer, we came here to view the cottage?'

'You kept the keys?' I gasped.

'Surely you didn't expect me to go all the way back into Helston that day — in the pouring rain too? And besides, Kati was with me, simmering nicely.'

'You're despicable!' I snapped. 'Get out. There's no way you're staying here a minute longer.'

'Come now, darling. Just take a look outside. Snow, frost, ice. You wouldn't send a dog out in that, would you? No, my darling. Here I am and here I stay. We're just going to have a merry little Christmas together, whatever you feel about it.'

13

Jonathan was right. Snow was falling heavily now, whirling against the window and beginning to cover the garden. I wondered whether Matthew would be able to reach Tolruan — the lanes were narrow, high-banked and twisting. Drifts would soon form, blocking them.

'Look, Zannah, we'll have to make the best of things. I'm here whether you like it or not.'

'But why?' I asked. 'What made you come down here?'

'You, Zannah.' Jonathan's grey eyes met mine candidly. 'Whatever you may think of me, I still love you — and want you. You must realise by now that I don't give up easily.'

'Surely you haven't driven nearly three hundred miles on Christmas Day just to tell me that, Jonathan,' I observed scornfully.

'What about something to eat?' he said, adroitly changing the subject. 'I brought you a Harrods hamper as a present, so that should keep us going for a day or so.'

As I'd already cooked a chicken, I sliced it and made a pile of sandwiches, while Jonathan uncorked a bottle of wine. Outside the wind was rising, the snow still falling, but with a log fire blazing up the chimney, sending out clouds of sparks as the wood settled, I began to relax slightly. Jonathan was right, we were stuck with each other. It was best not to let his company irk me.

'Why don't you forget him, Zannah?' Jonathan's voice was persuasive, or maybe it was the mellowing effect of the wine. 'He's an unpredictable sort of guy, isn't he? And that nursing-home is the most important thing in his life. Nothing else can compete with it — not even you.'

I knew Jonathan's words were true.

Tolruan must always come first with Matthew, but did it matter? I loved him. And I loved Tolruan too. It was part of Matthew.

Jonathan knelt to put another log on the fire. Resin slowly seeped out, creeping down into the glowing embers, and a smell of pine began to fill the room. He leaned back, resting his fair head against my knees and for a second I was tempted to stroke the soft thatch of smooth hair, as I had done so many times before. Our closeness pulsed in the growing warmth.

'What do you know about Matthew Tregenna?'

'Know?' I was startled by the question. 'He's a doctor and runs Tolruan. Why?' I said, realising how little I did know.

'What about his past? Has he always lived here? Does he have a family? Has he ever been married? After all, he must be in his early thirties.'

A wife — the thought had never occurred to me.

'Most men of that age have been married.'

I considered Jonathan's words, trying to remember what Matthew had told me, not that we'd spent much time alone together.

'This Hugh . . . the boy who used to stay with your Aunt Lucy . . . tell me about him. Where did he come from? How old was he? What did he look like?'

'It's all so long ago, Jonathan,' I protested wearily.

'Come on now, Zannah. You must remember. He was a great part of your life, wasn't he?'

I forced my mind back, searching.

'We used to stay here . . . with Aunt Lucy. For as long as I can remember, Hugh was always there. Thin, dark, but oh so distant and withdrawn. Aunt Lucy explained that his mother had re-married and he didn't like his new stepfather. I remember that Hugh was always aggressive, hating everything and everyone, but it didn't matter somehow

— I loved him. We both did — Aunt Lucy and I.'

'What was his surname?'

'Taylor. Hugh Taylor,' I answered.

'Was that his own name or the name he took when his mother re-married?'

'I've no idea. His own, I suppose. I don't even know his new father's name. Why?'

'Can't you see? Things are beginning to form a pattern, Zannah. When was the last time you saw Hugh?'

'I can't remember. Years ago. He stopped visiting Aunt Lucy when I was there. I must have been about twelve or thirteen. Hugh was five years older. He was going up to university.'

'University?' Jonathan's voice was alert. 'What did he study?'

'Oh really, Jonathan! How should I know? I told you, I didn't see him again. Some form of biology, I believe. He was always interested in that kind of thing. Always searching for creatures in the rock pools and wandering the seashore with bits of trailing seaweed.

Does it matter?'

'It might.'

Placing another log on the fire, Jonathan flopped down on the sofa beside me, the softness of his thick sweater brushing my cheek as his arm slid along the back of the seat, his fingers resting lightly on my shoulder. 'Are you sure Hugh didn't study medicine?' he asked softly.

'Could be.' Then the meaning of his words came to me and I stared disbelievingly at him. 'What are you saying?'

'I'm beginning to wonder more and more about your beloved Hugh — and Matthew Tregenna. Suppose they are the same man?'

'Don't be ridiculous, Jonathan,' I laughed. 'How could they be?'

'It's not so stupid, Zannah. Thin, dark, withdrawn, interested in living creatures . . . it all fits.'

'Aunt Lucy did always shorten names,' I said, suddenly remembering. 'She called me Zannah instead of Suzannah.'

'And Hugh, or Hew, instead of Matthew,' Jonathan cried triumphantly. 'If his stepfather's name was Tregenna and he took that, then Matthew Tregenna could easily be Hugh Taylor.'

'But he can't be. I would have recognised him.'

'Why should you? A teenage boy can change a great deal in twelve or more years.' Jonathan looked thoughtfully at me. 'That will of your aunt's, do you have it?'

'Yes,' I replied, getting up. 'Mr. Danvers gave me a photocopy. It's in the bureau.'

I opened the desk top and rummaged through a collection of papers tucked inside, selecting one long envelope which I gave to Jonathan.

He pulled out the thick paper inside and began to read it aloud:

'I, LUCY MABEL PARTINGTON of Lavender Cottage Lizard Point in the Duchy of Cornwall HEREBY REVOKE all former Wills and Testamentary Dispositions made by me and DECLARE

THIS to be my last Will.

'One. I DESIRE that my body be cremated and my ashes scattered over the sea near my home.

'Two. I GIVE DEVISE AND BEQUEATH all my residuary estate whatsoever or wheresoever situate after the payment of my just debts funeral and testamentary expenses to be divided between my beloved niece SUZANNAH EDGECUMBE and my late husband's nephew HUGH TAYLOR in equal shares absolutely and if one shall pre-decease the other then the whole of my residuary estate shall pass to the survivor for his or her own use absolutely . . . '

Jonathan stopped and looked at me thoughtfully. 'So if one of you dies, the other inherits the whole estate. Your Aunt Lucy was quite wealthy, wasn't she?'

'Yes, she was. I didn't realise but she'd dabbled on the stock exchange for years and made quite a fortune. From the quiet way she lived, I thought she had very little money, but it just went on growing and growing.'

'Tolruan needs quite a packet to keep it running . . . '

'Are you suggesting that it was Matthew who threw me over the cliff?' I cried incredulously. 'Oh, Jonathan, I know you dislike him, but don't you think you're letting your imagination run away with you?'

'Not at all,' Jonathan replied firmly. 'If Matthew Tregenna is Hugh Taylor, then it fits. With you out of the way, Aunt Lucy's fortune is all his and Tolruan goes on. Of course, half a fortune would keep it running for a while, but Doctor Tregenna is quite fanatical about the place, isn't he? A while wouldn't be enough. It has to be for ever, so far as he's concerned.'

'That really is too far-fetched, Jonathan. I've never heard such nonsense! As if Matthew would push anyone over a cliff. And, if you were right, what about all the happenings at

Tolruan while we were filming that documentary?'

'He was trying to divert suspicion.'

'Setting fire to Tolruan?' I said scornfully.

'One room and a lot of smoke. There was more panic than fire, don't forget.'

'Matthew wouldn't upset his patients like that,' I protested.

'He's a desperate man, Zannah, fighting to save his little kingdom.'

'And drowning Barbara's dog? And shooting that poor film extra? Matthew just wouldn't do that. It's right against his nature and, anyway, what would be the point?'

'Diverting suspicion, as I said before. People would think that if there was someone so unbalanced at large, doing these horrific things — that same person could easily have thrown you over the cliff as well.'

'Really, Jonathan! You should be writing fiction, not me,' I remarked, but the seeds of doubt were sewn, weaving their way into my brain, making me wonder.

I glanced at my watch. 'It's nearly two o'clock and I'm exhausted. You can sleep on the sofa down here.'

'When there's that beautiful four-poster waiting upstairs?'

Jonathan's arm slid along my shoulders, his fingers caressing the base of my neck.

'You are sleeping down here,' I repeated firmly. 'I'll bring you some blankets.'

'Now who's being far-fetched, Zannah?' Jonathan's hands slipped down my back, pulling me against him, his mouth moving towards mine. 'Why do you think I came all this way? Not to sleep on a sofa in front of the fire.'

'When are you going to understand that I don't love you any more, Jonathan?'

'Who said anything about love?' His fingers were tangling into my hair, drawing my face to his as he spoke. 'I want you, Zannah. Every moment of the day and night, I want you — that's why I'm here. Can't you understand? You're part of me and I'm not letting you go ever again.'

I felt for the door handle behind me and reached out to open it, wrenching myself free from Jonathan's grip, then slammed it in his face, turning the key. I could hear his fists pounding against the wood as I ran up the stairs and shut the door behind me, throwing myself on my bed in a flood of tears, until finally, worn out by a day full of emotion, I slept.

★   ★   ★

Snow edged the windows when I woke, stiff and cold. I looked down over the whiteness that reached to the cliff-edge, where tussocks of grass were buried under its weight, seeing the sea, flat and grey under a heavy sky, stretching far into the distance.

Going downstairs, I unlocked the living-room door. Jonathan lay, deeply asleep, on the sofa, his long limbs overhanging its arms, his chin dark with stubble, his hair ruffled — and for a moment I still loved him, remembering how once I'd felt about him. How once we would have been together, deep in that four-poster bed of Aunt Lucy's, deep in our love for each other. But not any more.

And I remembered Matthew.

Could Jonathan be right? Was it possible that Matthew and Hugh were the same man? The whole idea was quite ridiculous. I took eggs and bacon from the fridge and began to prepare breakfast.

The snow had stopped falling now and thin watery sunshine lightened the sky, filling the garden with sparkling radiance. A robin left a trail of delicate footprints across the lawn in its search for crumbs. Voices chattered as people began to walk along the cliff-top, destroying the perfection of the snow.

Jonathan came into the kitchen. 'I'm going back to London, Zannah. There's no point in staying, is there? You're not going to change, whatever I say.'

'I'm sorry, Jonathan.'

I was truly sorry. Sorry for all that had once been, and could never be again. The words seemed so inadequate. I knew, now, what it was like to love deeply and receive nothing in return.

'Before you go . . . tell me the truth . . . was it you? All those accidents at Tolruan? Tell me. Please. I have to know.'

Jonathan nodded. 'I hate him, Zannah,' he replied quite simply. 'I really hate him — and you love him so much. I wanted to destroy everything he cared about and by doing so, destroy him. Not that anyone could prove a thing about what happened — I made damn sure of that — so don't try running to the police with any tales.'

He ran distracted fingers through his untidy hair. 'What's the point? What does it matter any more? You'll never come back to me, will you, Zannah?

I've been offered a job in America. That's why I came here — to see you and persuade you to come with me. But there's no hope of that any more, is there?'

I shook my head, reaching up to pull his face down to mine and kissed him gently on the lips, drawing away before his passion could grow and overwhelm me.

'Goodbye, Jonathan.'

★   ★   ★

The cottage had a strange silence after he'd gone. Surrounded by the snow, everything had an unearthly quality, a stillness, a hushed almost reverent feeling. The path along the cliffs was empty now, trodden into dark muddiness by dozens of feet. Spoilt. Sullied.

A lone gull hovered low against the greyness of the sky, almost motionless. Was this what I really wanted? This solitude. This loneliness.

⋆ ⋆ ⋆

I had to put the time to use and soon my typewriter was clattering with an abundance of words. Loneliness has to be compensated and I peopled my days with characters, black words on paper, and watched the countryside begin to slowly change as the weeks grew into spring.

Kati was a frequent visitor, keeping me up-to-date with all that happened at Tolruan. Her talk seemed always to be about Helga Svensen and Matthew Tregenna — telling me things I didn't want to hear.

'She'll marry him — everyone says so. They're going away together next weekend. Some conference or other in London. That'll be it, I reckon. The final knot tied. He'll marry her then. Doctor Tregenna is always so proper, isn't he? He's sure to do the right thing.'

Why should I care, I thought. But I did. I cared very much.

'Both away at the same time?' I queried.

'Oh, Doctor Tregenna didn't want to leave Tolruan, but Doctor Svensen persuaded him. She's arranged for someone else — from the hospital in Barnstaple — to take over. Very good at arranging things, she is. Too good.' Kati's shrewd brown eyes flickered over me. 'Don't you mind?'

'Mind? Why should I, Kati?'

'I always thought you rather fancied Doctor Tregenna.'

I'd forgotten how observant Kati was.

'Did you?' I said, trying to keep my voice casual.

'And that he was keen on you too. All those trips to the beach. He never did that sort of thing before you came.'

'Didn't he?' I was surprised, remembering what Matthew had said when we went to the Lizard for the first time. 'I thought Doctor Tregenna swam quite often.'

'Oh, he did. But not miles away like

213

that. He used the swimming pool at Tolruan. It was only when you came that he took a whole afternoon off. Everyone noticed,' she said smugly. 'They all thought . . . '

'What, Kati?'

'Well, you know . . . that you and he . . .' Her voice trailed away. 'Only now it's Doctor Svensen.'

After Kati had gone, I kept thinking about what she'd said. Matthew and Helga in London. Together.

As the days passed and the weekend grew closer, the thought bothered me more and more. It made me angry. Why should it matter to me what Matthew chose to do? I didn't care, did I? Did I?

★ ★ ★

Saturday dawned with a red sky. Shepherd's warning, I thought, looking out at its glory reflected on the crinkling surface of the sea. A whisper of wind blew my curtains gently.

By the time I went out for a walk, the

wind had grown in intensity, coming in great forceful gusts over the sea, bending the trees low, filling the air with salt.

I fought my way back up the path, noticing how daffodils and narcissi were sending up stiff straight buds and hoped the gale wouldn't snap them off before they even had a chance to bloom.

Switching on the light, I began to type, disturbed by the constant rattle of windows, hearing rose-stems tap against the panes, doors creak eerily as if the cottage was taking on a life of its own.

By the time I went to bed the sea was thundering against the cliffs, vibrating the whole cottage. The gale had risen to full force, shrieking and whistling down the chimney, sending spatters of soot into the grate.

In the darkness something crashed and I got up to check the windows again, peering through the mist of salt hazing them in an attempt to see outside. An apple tree near the house leaned sideways, one thick branch hanging, swaying to and fro.

With a clatter, a tile slid down the roof and landed on the path, shattering. I stood, petrified, waiting for the chimney to follow. If the stack came through . . .

Deciding to get dressed, I went downstairs. At least I could run into the garden if the walls began to crumble.

It was like a nightmare now, the sea hurling itself with such force against the cliffs that I was terrified they would crumble, taking the cottage with them. How far was it from the cliff-edge? Only yards. I'd seen huge sections, fallen over the years, reaching down to the beach on my many walks, never even thinking about how it had happened.

Now, any minute, the same thing could happen here.

If I went outside, I too could be blown over the edge.

I sat on the sofa beside the dying

embers of the fire, clutching Aunt Lucy's rose-coloured eiderdown round me for comfort, remembering how I'd clung to her, in the safety of that old four-poster bed upstairs, Hugh perched, white-faced, on the chair beside us.

If only she was here now.

Suddenly I realised the thundering outside had acquired a pattern, knocking at regular intervals, and somewhere outside a voice was shouting. Running to the door, I opened it, thrown back against the wall by the force of the wind as it swirled in.

'Zannah! Are you all right?'

Matthew stood there, dark hair flattened to his head, raindrops trickling down the worried lines of his face.

Together we pushed the door shut, then he pulled off his dripping raincoat and wellingtons, leaving a trail of water over the hall floor.

'I thought you were in London,' I gasped weakly, still trembling. 'Kati said . . . '

'Still the little gossip,' he grinned, pushing back his wet hair and guiding me into the warmth of the living room. 'With that weather forecast, I didn't want to leave Tolruan. Helga's gone on her own. She's far more dedicated to this kind of thing than I am. Very ambitious.'

'But you have left Tolruan to come here,' I reminded him.

'I was worried about you on your own.'

'And Tolruan?' I questioned.

'There's a fellow from Barnstaple . . . sensible sort of chap.'

'You mean you actually put me first?'

Matthew's thin face broke into a smile. 'You always come first in my thoughts.'

'Do I?' I asked in surprise.

The storm still raged violently around us, but somehow, now, it didn't matter. Matthew was here in Aunt Lucy's cottage with me. And I was safe, once more held in the closeness of comforting arms.

14

The storm had died down a little when the first strands of daylight began to brighten the sky. Matthew and I went out into the garden to see what damage it had caused.

Several apple-tree branches lay shattered on the ground and the lavender bushes were almost flattened by the force of the gale. There were gaps on the roof where some of the ridge tiles had lifted, sliding down onto the lawn. Apart from that, the cottage had weathered the gale as it had done many times before over the years.

Further along the cliff-path a huge section had broken away, yawning like a wide mouth into the wind-blown grass along its edge.

I gazed at Matthew, seeing that thick dark hair falling over the deep blue of his eyes, those thin handsome features;

knowing that far-away look so well.

And Jonathan's words haunted me. Could he really be Hugh?

'I want to go back,' I said, catching hold of his sleeve.

'Go back where?' he asked, puzzled.

'To where I fell — that ledge. It's the only way, Matthew. The only way I'll ever know what happened.'

He regarded me doubtfully. 'I'm not so sure, Zannah. Seeing it all again . . . it might not be a good thing.'

'But I've got to know. It's the one missing piece. Those final hours. Someone threw me over that cliff, Matthew. I have to remember why — and who.'

With great reluctance, he finally agreed, but whether because he feared what might happen to my mind — or that I would discover something terrible, I didn't know.

'Now, Matthew. I want to go now,' I insisted urgently. 'Right away.'

Pulling on my coat, I hurried to the door with Matthew following more slowly, and ran along the muddy track, feeling the wind tug at my clothes, biting icily into my cheeks.

Matthew drove carefully down the lanes, avoiding fallen branches, his face grim, and as he did I watched every movement he made, trying to remember.

Were those the same blue eyes, so often hidden from me by a thick fringe of hair? Had that narrow anxious face now widened into handsome maturity; the skinny body broadened and grown tall? Hugh's remote and lonely manner was so like that of Matthew as if, at times, hiding himself from the rest of the world.

'You're quite sure you know what you're doing, Zannah?' Matthew asked, glancing sideways at me, the lines on his face etched deep, his eyes haunted. 'The mind is a strange thing. It can snap so easily. Your memory has to return at its own pace. Forcing it could cause harm. I'm not certain you're ready for this.'

Grey clouds scudded across the sky, whipped by the wind into long trailing mares' tails. Trees leaned sideways, their branches quivering. The grass lay, beaten almost flat. White horses flecked the heaving surface of the sea in the distance as the car wove its way, winding and twisting, between the high banks of the narrow lanes.

Matthew's knuckles were white as he gripped the steering wheel tightly, his face a mask of tension.

'How will you know where to find the exact place?' I questioned.

'I'll know. I've been there before.'

With me? I wondered.

★ ★ ★

The full force of the wind met us as we reached the cliff-top, swaying the car with its strength. Matthew climbed out, his jacket billowing around him, and tugged at my door, fighting to hold it open. As I stepped onto the springy turf, my breath was snatched away making me gasp.

Clutching his arm tightly, I battled my way towards the edge, seeing the waves, whipped high into plumes of spray, crash against the darkness of the rocks. It was beginning to rain again, stinging our cheeks like the flail of a whip.

Matthew stopped and turned towards me. I'd never seen such torment on a man's face before.

Or was it guilt?

With a feeling of foreboding, I wondered why I'd come.

If Matthew and Hugh were the same man, what would happen now? If Matthew had thrown me over that cliff once, why not again? And yet I had to know.

My heart was pounding, thundering in my ears like the sea far below, as we reached the very edge of the cliff, almost leaning against the strength of the wind.

'Look down, Zannah,' Matthew whispered. 'Look down and remember, if you must.'

I bent forward, gazing past the flat surface of the wet cliff-face. Against huge tumbled rocks scattered at the bottom, waves lashed, rising up every now and then as if hungry, hiding them in a flurry of white foam.

I licked my dry lips, tasting the salt.

Far below was a shelf of rock, so small I could hardly believe it had held me, preventing me from falling further. Tussocks of grass grew there, green and thick.

A shiver crept up my spine.

'Now do you remember?'

I shook my head, bewildered and buffeted by the storm, my hair whirling round me, stinging into my tear-wet eyes.

'Think back, Zannah. Think.'

. . . 'Zannah! After so many years! You're quite beautiful.' Hugh's blue eyes smiled into mine.

Delighted, I lifted my face to kiss his cheek and felt him draw back, his whole body stiffening.

'It's a pleasant hotel,' I said,

desperate to make some form of contact with him.

Hugh, my beloved Hugh. For how long had I dreamed of him and only him, my whole life coloured by that picture? Every man I met had to stand comparison with an idol — and every man so far had failed.

'We have to see the solicitor.' Hugh's voice was tense. 'There's not much time.' He glanced at his watch impatiently. 'Do you want tea?'

'No, it can wait,' I said. 'Our appointment's at four o'clock. Shall we go now?'

Hugh seemed on edge, jumpy — or maybe he was always like that. As we climbed the steep street I looked at him, trying to visualise the sad, lonely little boy I'd known and loved. He'd altered so much.

'Where do you live now, Hugh?' I asked, wanting to penetrate that hard shell-like barrier between us.

'Live? Oh, here and there. I travel abroad quite a bit.'

'As part of your job?' I questioned.

'Still curious, still asking questions. You haven't changed, Mermaid.'

I'd forgotten that name. Mermaid. Hugh always called me that, ever since he'd seen me swimming in the sea that day, my hair floating around me. It was the only sign of affection he'd ever shown.

Mr. Danvers welcomed us, sitting us down, fussing round. Aunt Lucy was a rich woman. We were important clients.

Carefully he explained her will.

'Divided equally . . . unless one of us should die?' Hugh queried.

'Then the whole estate reverts to the surviving beneficiary,' confirmed Mr. Danvers.

'I never realised Aunty Lucy had so much money,' I breathed, still recovering from the surprise.

'She was a very astute woman,' smiled Mr. Danvers. 'Investing her money wisely and living very simply herself. Her capital grew. Even divided between you, the sum is quite vast.'

'Quite vast,' repeated Hugh.

★   ★   ★

We ate together in the hotel that night.

'A celebration, Mermaid,' Hugh smiled, holding up his glass.

'Not a celebration, Hugh,' I said sadly. 'Aunt Lucy is dead, remember.'

'A celebration to our new wealth then.'

Somehow I couldn't celebrate that.

'How about a walk?' Hugh announced unexpectedly, pushing back his chair. 'After a meal like that I need some fresh air. Come on.'

'I'll have to change out of this dress,' I replied. 'And these high heels aren't made for walking far either.'

'Hurry then.' He seemed suddenly impatient.

Wearing a lavender-blue tee-shirt and jeans I ran down the stairs. Hugh was nowhere to be seen, but eventually I found him him pacing up and down the pavement by his car.

'We'll go out to the Lizard, shall we? See Aunt Lucy's cottage maybe? I've almost forgotten what it looks like after all these years,' Hugh suggested.

He held open the door and I climbed in, glad to be alone with him at last.

'Must we really sell Aunt Lucy's cottage, Hugh?' I asked, as he drove carefully down the narrow lanes. 'It holds so many happy memories.'

'Happy? For you maybe. Suzannah, the beloved and cherished child. Mine are somewhat different.' His voice was harsh.

'I'm sorry, Hugh. I'd forgotten,' I said. 'But the time with Aunt Lucy was always happy, wasn't it? Even for you? She was so full of love.'

'It only made the comparison worse. My whole childhood was a torment. A father I'd loved — and lost. A mother I wanted so much to love, but whom I had to share with a man I hated. Aunt Lucy . . . and you.'

'What about me, Hugh?' I prompted,

needing to know that he loved me too.

'You were always there, clinging on like a limpet, forcing your way relentlessly into my life.'

I couldn't believe the bitterness.

'But, Hugh . . .'

He jolted the car to a halt and I looked at him, sitting tensely beside me, wanting to hold him close, dispel the torment filling his eyes, but he didn't speak, just sat there, staring far away into the distance. I'd seen that same expression so often before when we were children.

'I've always loved you, Hugh,' I said quietly.

'Loved me!' The scorn in his voice made me flinch. 'You!'

He opened the car door and pulled me out, his fingers gripping my arm. 'And I've always hated you.'

I stood still, staring back at him, unable to believe his words.

'Aunt Lucy always loved you best. Her precious niece. Her flesh and blood. I was her husband's nephew, no relation at all. She never let me forget it.'

'That's not true!' I cried, stung into anger, stumbling as he hurried me over the grass towards the cliff-top. 'Aunt Lucy treated us both the same, loving us equally. Think of her will, Hugh. Equal shares.'

'She was always talking about you, Zannah. What you'd achieved. Your latest programme on TV. How proud she was every time she saw your name on the screen.'

'You came to see her?' I questioned. 'I didn't realise that.'

'Frequently, especially when she was so ill. But you . . . you deserted her. Never came near. All those days she was in hospital, you didn't visit once.'

His nails bit into my arm as we stood there, right by the edge, swaying in the force of the wind.

'I didn't know, Hugh. When I saw her — oh, six or seven weeks before she died, she looked so frail, almost transparent, but she insisted she was

230

quite all right. Nothing wrong at all. Just arthritis, she said, giving her so much pain. That's why she had to rest, she told me. And I believed her, Hugh. Aunt Lucy never lied.'

'She was dying of cancer.' His words were like a whiplash.

'I know that now, Hugh. But I didn't then. Truly I didn't. I wanted to cancel my trip to Ethiopia, let someone else do it, but she became quite angry at the idea. Insisting I went. It was such a wonderful chance, she said. She made me promise, Hugh. And when you made Aunt Lucy a promise, you didn't break it, did you?'

'You didn't come to her funeral, Zannah. Or even send a wreath of flowers.'

'How could I, Hugh? I didn't know. I was in Ethiopia. Out there we were totally cut off,' I explained. 'That was the whole point of the documentary. Showing areas no one had even seen before. We lived with the people. Like them. It was the only way to experience and understand their suffering.'

I tried to move away, feeling Hugh's grip on my arms tighten.

'I only learned about Aunt Lucy's death when I returned home. Then it was too late. I came down here straight away. You know that.'

'She was still talking about you, right up to the end. Zannah, her precious Zannah. And yet, I was the one there beside her.'

'But that was Aunt Lucy, Hugh. When I saw her, she always talked about you, telling me what a success you were, how well you were doing at university. I think she just wanted to keep us up-to-date with each other. We never met, did we?'

'I made damn sure of that!' His blue eyes were like chips of ice, glaring out from his gaunt, angular face. 'I worshipped her. She was the one stable thing in my life. And yet she only cared about you. I was throwing away my love, once again. First my father, then my mother, and then Aunt Lucy, loving only you. All the love I've ever tried to give, has been tossed back in my face.'

'You're so wrong, Hugh. I love you.'

As I spoke, I felt a surge of shock, seeing the terrible hatred that flared in his blazing eyes. This was the man I'd loved for all those years. The romantic image I'd held in my heart.

This vicious, bitter man.

His face was close to mine, his eyes burning, his thin lips twisted into a travesty of a smile, and he laughed, a mirthless sound.

'To be divided equally . . . unless one shall predecease the other.'

His hands were forcing me backwards now, nearer and nearer to the cliff-edge. I felt my feet slip on the softness of the grass, sensing the void stretching behind me, hearing the waves pound over those cruel rocks.

'Now, Zannah, you're going to pay me back . . . '

'No!' I screamed . . .

★   ★   ★

'No!' I screamed, struggling in the clasp of Matthew's strong arms as they closed round me, drawing me away from that terrible void.

'It's all right, Zannah,' he soothed gently. 'You're quite safe now.'

'Oh, Matthew,' I sobbed, letting him lead me back to the car. 'It was Hugh . . . and then . . . '

Too vividly I could remember it all now, falling, falling.

Hugh's fingers desperately clutching at me as he fell too. Then the horrible jolt as I hit the ledge and Hugh . . . I could still hear the echo of his scream floating in the surging sea-salt air. Bodies are rarely found in those treacherous depths. Would Hugh's ever be?

'Oh, Zannah.' Matthew's lips brushed mine, his eyes full of sadness. 'I shouldn't have brought you back here.'

I shook my head, leaning against the tweed of his jacket, feeling the comfort of its roughness against my cheek. 'I had to know. And . . . you're not Hugh, are you?'

'Me?' The hidden twinkle in his blue eyes sparkled into life. 'How could I be?'

'It was just something Jonathan said. And you do fit the image.'

'I love you, Zannah.' The words were muffled in my hair.

I pulled away, smiling up at him. 'Tell me again, Matthew.'

'I love you, Zannah. I always have and always will.'

'More than Tolruan?' I challenged mischievously.

'More than anything.'

'And what about Helga?'

'Helga?'

'Kati says . . . '

Matthew's blue eyes laughed into mine. 'Kati says . . . ' he mimicked.

'Well, that Helga and you . . . '

'Helga Svensen is a very ambitious woman, Zannah. She's only using Tolruan to improve her experience.'

'In what way?' I commented drily.

'Do I detect a hint of jealousy?'

'Of course not,' I protested. 'Well . . . maybe just a little.'

My words died away as Matthew kissed me.

'And now what?' I said, when I could breathe again.

'I'd like to marry you as soon as possible.'

My heart sang with happiness.

'But there's just one thing that prevents me . . . you're a wealthy woman, Zannah.'

'Does it matter? I love you, Matthew. Nothing else matters. Oh, the money will be useful, I don't deny that. It means Tolruan is safe now. That would've pleased Aunt Lucy, I know. Money isn't important to me, but you are — and Tolruan.'

A harebell quivered, fragile and blue. Seagulls hovered on silent wings. I could hear the sound of waves pounding. Drifts of spray misted my cheeks, mingling with the rain.

Matthew's arms were crushing me as

if he'd never let me go, his lips burning mine and I knew that whatever happened, nothing would ever part us again.

Here, at last, I'd found the answers. Now life could begin again for me, for Matthew and for Tolruan.

We do hope that you have enjoyed reading this large print book.

Did you know that all of our titles are available for purchase?

We publish a wide range of high quality large print books including:
Romances, Mysteries, Classics
General Fiction
Non Fiction and Westerns

Special interest titles available in large print are:
The Little Oxford Dictionary
Music Book, Song Book
Hymn Book, Service Book

Also available from us courtesy of Oxford University Press:
Young Readers' Dictionary
(large print edition)
Young Readers' Thesaurus
(large print edition)

For further information or a free brochure, please contact us at:
Ulverscroft Large Print Books Ltd.,
The Green, Bradgate Road, Anstey,
Leicester, LE7 7FU, England.
Tel: (00 44) **0116 236 4325**
Fax: (00 44) **0116 234 0205**

A TEMPORARY AFFAIR

Carol MacLean

Cass Bryson is persuaded by her twin sister Lila to attend a celebrity party in her stead, accompanying the enigmatic photographer Finn Mallory. Then, when his secretary falls ill, he asks Cass to take over her job temporarily. Though she can't deny her attraction to her new boss, Cass is lacking in self-confidence, not least because of the scars she bears from a tragic accident. But Finn is drawn to Cass too, and it seems they might just find love together — until Lila returns, determined to capture his heart for herself . . .

THE RUBY

Fay Cunningham

Cass finds her friend Michael dead in his swimming pool, and while drowning appears at first to be the cause, evidence mounts that foul play was involved. The investigation brings the handsome Detective Inspector Noel Raven into Cass's life — and the connection between the two is literally electrifying. Cass's mother, a witch, warns her that she may be in deadly danger; only by working together can Cass and Noel hope to overcome the evil forces at work. Though Cass finds that her gemstones are also handy in a pinch . . .

FRANCESCA

Susan Udy

When her sister Francesca disappears, Jamie is determined to unravel the truth. Keeping her identity a secret, she inveigles her way into the household where Francesca lived with her husband, the compelling Alexander Whittaker: wildlife expert, broadcaster — and Francesca's possible murderer. He was seen arguing with her just hours before she vanished, and evidence mounts up that he knew she'd been having an affair. Playing detective becomes a dangerous game for Jamie, especially when she realises she has lost her heart to the prime suspect . . .

BENEATH AN OUTBACK SKY

Noelene Jenkinson

Sophie Nash's outback pastoral station in South Australia's panoramic Flinders Ranges is in danger of going under, unless she can find another source of revenue. So when charismatic geologist Charlie Kendall arrives to camp on her property with his students, love is the last thing on her mind. In fact, Sophie has seen personal loss devastate her family and has vowed never to lose her heart. But Charlie's charms are hard to resist, and his family might just have the solution to her problems . . .